## "Will you trust me?"

She nodded. At this point he was the only one she could trust. No one else had been willing to help her.

Only Jasper.

His pupils had definitely grown bigger. They almost swallowed the green of his eyes. "Good." Then his fingers were under her chin. His head was bending toward her.

Was he...was he about to kiss her?

"I won't let you get hurt," he promised. His voice was rough and dark, the way she thought it would sound when he was in bed with a woman. Whispering in the night.

Her gaze fell to his mouth.

She wanted him to kiss her.

*I want to kiss him.* Maybe it was the adrenaline and the fear still pumping through her. Whatever it was, in that one instant Veronica felt a little bit wild.

*USA TODAY* Bestselling Author

# CYNTHIA EDEN

# GUARDIAN RANGER

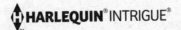 HARLEQUIN® INTRIGUE®

I want to offer a huge thank-you to my readers! Your support is so
amazing—thank you! I hope you enjoy this installment of my Shadow
Agents series. I sure had a wonderful time writing this tale.

Recycling programs
for this product may
not exist in your area.

ISBN-13: 978-0-373-74725-2

GUARDIAN RANGER

Copyright © 2013 by Cynthia Roussos

Printed in U.S.A.

www.Harlequin.com

# ABOUT THE AUTHOR

*USA TODAY* bestselling author Cynthia Eden writes tales of romantic suspense and paranormal romance. Her books have received starred reviews from *Publishers Weekly*, and she has received a RITA® Award nomination for best romantic suspense. Cynthia lives in the deep South, loves horror movies and has an addiction to chocolate. More information about Cynthia may be found on her website, www.cynthiaeden.com, or you can follow her on Twitter (www.twitter.com/cynthiaeden).

## Books byCynthia Eden

HARLEQUIN INTRIGUE
1398—ALPHA ONE*
1404—GUARDIAN RANGER*

*Shadow Agents

# CAST OF CHARACTERS

**Jasper Adams**—An ex-army ranger, Jasper is working undercover for the EOD (Elite Operations Division) in order to track down a killer. His problem? He never expected to fall for the suspect's sister, and as the danger grows around Veronica, guarding her suddenly becomes his top priority.

**Veronica Lane**—Veronica is desperate to find her missing brother, and when she hires Jasper to help her locate Cale, Veronica thinks she's finally discovered a savior. But before they can find Cale, Veronica is put in the crosshairs of a killer.

**Cale Lane**—*Dangerous. Deadly.* Those two words normally describe the army ranger, but has he crossed the line and become a killer? The bodies are piling up, and all the evidence says that Cale is dead guilty.

**Wyatt Halliday**—The local sheriff moved from the big city to get away from all the violence and death, but now the small town of Whiskey Ridge seems to be under attack. If he's going to bring peace back to the area and protect the citizens, he'll have to work with the EOD.

**Jimmy Jones**—The young deputy is in way over his head, and, if he's not careful, he may not survive the nightmare that has just hit his quiet hometown.

**Gunner Ortez**—During his time as a SEAL sniper, Gunner became well acquainted with danger. He's willing to face any threat that comes his way, as long as he can keep Sydney Sloan safe.

**Sydney Sloan**—The mission should have been simple enough—use Veronica Lane to track her missing brother. But when more murders are committed, Sydney has to work up close and personal on this mission…with Gunner.

# Chapter One

Desperation had driven Veronica Lane to the small, run-down bar in the middle of absolute nowhere. That same desperation had her hands shaking and her heart racing as she pushed open the bar's old wooden doors and risked a cautious step inside Last Chance.

The bar name was rather fitting, but not exactly reassuring.

No band was playing in the bar. It wasn't that kind of place—no live bands would ever be playing in a joint like this. The interior was dim, and the bar smelled of alcohol and cigarettes. Despite its worn appearance, Last Chance was packed, mostly with men who were drinking and with some ladies who were dancing. Dancing to their own beat because the jukebox wasn't exactly spitting out any nice tunes.

Veronica felt unwanted eyes on her as she took another slow step inside the building. She knew her mark waited in that bar. She'd worked hard to track the man down. Now Veronica just had to convince him to help her.

*I can do this.*

She hoped.

The ridiculous high heels that she wore weren't exactly helping her to navigate or to look as though she knew what the heck she was doing. She'd tried to dress the part in order to fit in, but instead of giving her a sexy confidence, the short skirt she was wearing just made her feel exposed.

*Too many eyes.* The weight of all those stares was making her way too nervous.

After huffing out a hard breath, Veronica lifted her chin. *The bar.* She needed to head toward that long, thin, wooden counter with its assortment of stools. Didn't the bartender always know everything in places like this? He'd better. She dodged and weaved her way around the Last Chance patrons, then grabbed the bar countertop in a white-knuckled grip.

The bartender turned, the faint light gleaming off his bald head. A cowboy hat would cover that baldness.

He lifted a brow. "Want something?"

"A man."

Now both dark brows were up. Could she have sounded more like an idiot?

"His name's Jasper," she added. A name that didn't sound too dangerous, but the man…oh, yes, he was the most dangerous man she'd ever met. "Jasper Adams, and he's here."

The bartender pushed a whiskey glass toward a guy on the right. She saw the black ink of what appeared to be a skull tattoo peeking just beneath the sleeve of his shirt. He grunted, and her gaze jerked back up to meet his. "You sure you want to tangle with him?"

*No.* "Absolutely sure."

He smiled, and the smile just made his face look even harder. His dark eyes glinted as he said, "Then just follow the sound of fists."

The sound of…?

Then she heard the thud of fists. Unmistakable. A man shouted. Another growled. She even heard some cheers.

The bartender pointed toward the back room. "Have fun."

Doubtful.

Veronica sucked in a deep breath and followed the sound of voices and fists.

She had to push her way through the small crowd that had gathered at the back room. No bobbing or weaving this time. She had to *push* through a line of sweaty bodies. Cowboys who were enjoying one very brutal brawl.

Once she made it through that wall of bodies, Veronica saw what held the crowd so captivated. Two men were circling each other. One was tall, his body strong with muscles, his blond hair bright even in the dim light. The other man was pale, with a wild shot of red hair, black eyes and fists that moved so fast—

The blond male caught those fists in his hands. Just…caught them. Then he smiled. "Try harder next time." Then the big, blond fellow slammed his head into his opponent's face.

Veronica winced. She was pretty sure the red-head's nose had just broken.

The men around her cheered.

Veronica edged forward. She knew that blond male. Her hand lifted.

"Lady, what the hell?" Someone grabbed her hand and tried to haul her back.

The blond spun to face her, obviously ready for a sneak attack.

She smiled, hoping that she didn't look like a threat.

His eyes—a dark, deep green that she'd never been able to get out of her mind—narrowed on her. Then that green stare slowly swept over her face. Over her body. She warmed beneath his gaze.

Jasper Adams. Still just as big, bad and danger-ous as she remembered.

And just as sexy.

"You're gonna want to let her go," he murmured to the cowboy who held her. "And you're gonna want to do that right now."

The cowboy's hand instantly fell away from her.

Jasper didn't even glance back at the man behind her. His gaze had come back to meet Veronica's. "I...know you."

Though he didn't sound as if he actually remembered how he knew her. So much for making a lasting impression.

Jasper's gaze fell to the exposed length of her legs. "I'd like to know you even better."

Her face flushed. Maybe it was a good thing he was looking at her legs. That way, he missed the whole flaming-face bit.

Only his eyes were back on her face now, and he was almost smiling.

Time to take charge of the situation. Or try to. Veronica cleared her throat. "I need to talk with you, Jasper."

Since the man on the floor was crawling away now and holding his bleeding nose, the group started to thin. Jasper closed in on her. He reached for her hand. "Is that all you want?"

"No," she barely whispered.

She could tell by the heavy-lidded look in his eyes that Jasper had something more physical in mind. But even though she'd had a crush on him for more years than she wanted to confess, Veronica straightened her spine and said, "What I really want..."

He leaned in close to her. His heady scent—male, soap, the crisp outdoors—swept around her.

"What I really want…" She eased out a slow breath. "Is your help."

Judging by the expression on Jasper's handsome face, that was the last request he'd expected.

Jasper Adams. Ex-ranger. Lethal killing machine. Heartbreaker. Okay, those were the words whispered about him. She wasn't sure all of the rumors that she'd heard about him were true, and, right now, she didn't care.

One thing she did know…*ex-ranger* was the most important part to her. "I'm Veronica Lane." She said her name in case he'd forgotten, which he obviously had. "A few years ago, you were in a unit with my brother, Cale."

His eyelids flickered. Then he was pulling her deeper into the shadows. Pushing her toward a small wooden table that sat against the back of the bar. Privacy. A tiny bit of it, anyway.

"Do you remember him?" Veronica pressed.

Jasper rubbed his chin, studied her and nodded.

Her breath expelled in a relieved rush. "Good. He…he always spoke highly of you." *Spoke.* She'd used the past tense. That wasn't what she'd meant to do. Veronica blinked away the stupid tears that wanted to fill her eyes. "He said that you were one of the best trackers he knew."

"Is that all he said?" His voice, with the faintest hint of a Texas drawl, rolled over her.

"He said you were deadly. That I should…" This

part was embarrassing, but she wouldn't lie to him, so she finished, "He said that I should stay far away from a man like you."

Another slow nod. "Sounds about right." One golden brow rose. The man's face was almost perfect. Too gorgeous. High cheekbones. Square jaw. Firm lips. A slightly hawkish nose, but it just made his other features look even stronger. And his eyes...

A woman could easily be tempted by eyes like that. Tempted to do just about anything.

The jukebox started to play another tune. A slower song. The dance-with-me kind of song.

"If your brother warned you away, then why are you here, Ms. Veronica Lane?"

"Because I have to be." She perched on the edge of her chair. The chair's legs were uneven and wobbled a bit beneath her. "I need your help."

His fingertips drummed on the scarred tabletop. "And you think I'll help you because...?"

"Because I can pay you." She fumbled and opened her purse. "I even brought some cash in with me—"

He swore and grabbed her hands, closing the purse and trapping her fingers beneath his own. His skin was rough, the tips of his fingers and his palms calloused. "Lady, don't you know better than to flash a wad of cash in a bar like this?"

Her heart raced so fast that her chest hurt. "I'm desperate."

Very slowly, he released her. "Yes, ma'am," he drawled, "I am getting that impression."

"I heard…" Rumors, whispers, some of what she'd picked up from her brother over the years and some that she'd learned on her own. Clearing her throat, she said, "I heard that you would be willing to take on certain jobs if the money was right." She leaned forward. Her chair teetered. "I can make the money right for you, okay? Please." She wasn't above begging. *Because I am that desperate.* "Say you'll help me."

His eyes gave no clue to his thoughts. They were just a cold green shield. "What do you want me to do?" He waited a beat. "You trying to get me to kill someone for you?" His voice was silky soft, deadly.

She shook her head. "No, of course not!"

He just stared back at her. Veronica swallowed the lump in her throat. She realized that the "of course" probably didn't apply to him. He was ex-military, a man who often sold his lethal skills out to the highest bidder. Dealing out death…maybe that was common for him.

It wasn't so common for her.

Her fingers clenched around her purse strap. The better to hide the trembling of her hands. "I want you to *find* someone for me."

She caught the faintest expression of surprise in his gaze. A very, very fleeting expression.

"Who?" Jasper demanded.

"My brother. Cale's missing." Missing and, she feared, dead. Because Cale had been gone for six months. There'd been no contact at all from him during that time. Cale would never leave her for that long without a word. Even when he'd been working as an army ranger, he'd still found ways to check up on her. To let her know that he was alive.

Her brother knew how much she needed him. He wouldn't just leave her.

But Jasper leaned back in his chair and waved a dismissive hand. "Cale's a big boy. If any man knows how to take care of himself, it's him."

Why? Because her brother was a killer? A mercenary? Yes, she knew all the dark parts of Cale's life. It didn't make her love him less. Her chin lifted. "It's been six months. No calls. No letters. No texts or emails."

"He could be in deep cover. Maybe on a mission that can't be—"

"Cale didn't even tell me when he left." That was the part that had first tipped her off to the fact that something was wrong. "Before every mission, he always comes to see me." It was a ritual they'd had. After the sudden death of their parents, well, they'd needed to stick together. There hadn't been a choice. It had just been the two of them.

Cale had never gotten a chance to tell their parents goodbye, to say that he loved them that one final time.

So *every* time that Cale left for a mission, he came to see her. He always told her goodbye.

"He didn't tell me goodbye," she whispered.

Jasper shook his head. "You think your brother is missing because he didn't tell you goodbye?" He gave a low whistle. "I hate to break this to you, but—"

"Six. Months," she gritted, not about to be put off now. Fine, he could think she was crazy, but he'd still better take the job that she was offering to him. "If you don't believe me, well, you won't be the first. The local sheriff thinks I'm being neurotic, and he sure won't lift a finger to help me."

Jasper watched her with his steady gaze.

"Does it even matter if you believe me?" Veronica asked. "Can't you take the money, find him and then prove that I'm wrong? You'll get paid either way, I swear. I just need to know that he's alive." Because the gnawing in her gut told her that something was wrong.

She was afraid that Cale was dead.

"I can't live the rest of my life, wondering if my brother's body is in a shallow grave someplace. I need to know what's happened to him."

Jasper just kept staring back at her.

"Say *something,*" she told him, voice tight.

His head cocked to the right. "You're not what I expected."

Well, that was *something*. Just not what she'd wanted to hear.

"We met once, didn't we?" Jasper asked her.

So he remembered? She gave a quick nod.

His gaze narrowed on her. "Your hair's different."

Her hair didn't matter. Only Cale mattered. Why was Jasper stalling?

He said, "Your brother talked about you a lot. He was always telling me how smart you were."

Not so smart when it came to people. People generally made her feel lost, but when it came to computers and technology, she got by pretty well. "None of Jasper's credit cards have been used. None of his accounts touched. Not since he vanished."

"You know this because...?"

"Because it took me all of five minutes to get access to his accounts." With her computers, there was very little that she couldn't access. "If my brother had just been taking another job, then some cash should have been put in his account. A down payment, something. There was nothing."

"Maybe he gets paid when the job's done. Or maybe he has an account you don't know about." Jasper was being so calm and logical.

It was all she could do to stay seated. "There's always an up-front payment." *You don't risk your life for nothing*...that had been a Cale Lane rule. Rule number three, if she remembered correctly. "And I know about every account he has."

Jasper tapped his chin. She noticed that a faint growth of stubble covered his square jaw. The stubble made him look both dangerous and sexy.

She yanked her gaze away from that stubble and forced herself to look into his eyes once more. "You know him." She made her voice smooth with an effort. "He was your friend once. Please, take this job. I'll pay whatever you want."

"Whatever?"

She nodded.

His lashes flickered. "You should be careful making an offer like that. You don't know what I'll ask for. You don't know what kind of man I am."

"You're the kind of man I need." One with dark connections that could—hopefully—lead Veronica to her brother.

He studied her, and she fought the urge to squirm. After a moment, his lips slowly stretched into a smile. "Well, Ms. Veronica Lane, in that case, I think you've just hired yourself a mercenary."

An answering smile wanted to lift her lips because, for the first time in months, she could feel hope stirring inside her.

Jasper rose to his feet. She hurried to stand beside him. This close, she finally realized just how big he was. Jasper's shoulders stretched as wide as a linebacker's. "Thank you," she murmured, offering her hand.

His fingers closed around hers. "Don't thank me." The words sounded a little too gruff.

She glanced up, her brows pulling together.

His smile seemed forced. "I haven't found your brother yet."

"But you will." *Keep the hope. Don't let it fade.*

"Yes," Jasper said slowly, but with a definite promise rumbling beneath the words, "I will."

THE CROWD CLOSED in behind little Veronica Lane as she hurried away from him. Jasper watched her go, aware that his gaze had dropped to the curve of her hips.

The lady had one fine sway when she moved, even if she staggered a bit in those three-inch heels.

"Are you smiling?" The surprised question came from Jasper's left as Gunner Ortez grabbed a chair and swung it around. He sat down, looping his arms over the back of the chair. "Man, you know I've asked you not to do that. You're scary when you smile."

As if Gunner was one to talk. The ex-SEAL sniper just looked like one very deadly shark when he smiled.

"Was that who I think it was?" Gunner asked.

"If you mean was that Cale Lane's little sister, then, yes, it was." Talk about easy pickings. He'd been in town for less than five hours. He'd thought that he'd have to worm his way into Veronica's good graces before he could get a good start on this mission.

But the woman had just come walking right up to him.

"Want to tell me what she wanted?"

He and Gunner were working the assignment together, so there was no reason to hold back. "She just hired me to find her missing brother."

Not much could surprise Gunner. The guy had been to hell and back on his missions, but Jasper caught the faint flicker of surprise on his face. "You really have the devil's luck." Gunner saluted Jasper with a beer bottle.

"So they say." Sometimes it was hard to tell the difference between having luck and being cursed.

"You didn't tell her that you were EOD?"

Even if he'd told her, Jasper wasn't sure that Veronica would have even known about the group. Most civilians didn't know of its existence. "Have I ever broken cover?" Jasper tossed back at his friend.

Gunner shook his head.

"And I'm not starting now." As if a pretty face would sway him. Veronica had definitely been graced with a pretty face. Heart-shaped, with high cheeks, a round little nose and the biggest, brightest blue eyes he'd ever seen.

The eyes had caught his attention first, held it and made it hard for him to look away.

Then he'd noticed her mouth. Who would have

guessed that sweet Veronica Lane had a mouth made for sin?

Or legs that seemed to stretch forever.

He cleared his throat and shifted beneath the table. "As far as I can tell, the woman doesn't know a thing about the EOD. She thinks I'm a mercenary, just like Cale."

If she only knew the truth.

For the past two years, Jasper had been working for the Elite Operations Division. The hybrid group of ex-military personnel took on some damn dangerous missions...missions that no one else could handle. EOD agents generally worked off the grid. Way, way off.

But someone had started to hunt EOD agents. Three men had been killed in the past six months, and all signs were indicating that the killer was...

Cale Lane.

"So I guess you took the job?" Gunner asked.

"We came to an agreement." One that they'd hash out more later. "That agreement...it does involve me getting full access to Cale's house and all of his personal files."

"Lucky SOB," Gunner muttered, shaking his head.

Jasper shrugged. "He's missing. She wants me to find him." He still couldn't quite get over the shock of seeing her come for him, pushing out of the crowd, looking so out of place and so—

"What's going to happen when she finds out that you're in town to catch her brother? That Uncle Sam wants Cale locked up tight so that the man never sees daylight again?"

This time, Jasper's shrug was forced. "I guess she'll hate me then." Her blue eyes had flashed with so many emotions. Fear. Desperation. Hope.

Soon enough, he'd see what her gaze looked like when hate burned in those blue eyes.

"You're playing with fire." It was a warning that Gunner had given him before.

And, as before, Jasper's answer was the same. "Good thing I like to get burned." Then he rose from the table, and, because he was still thinking about her, still wondering about the lovely Ms. Veronica Lane, Jasper made his way out of the bar.

The EOD had already run a full background check on Veronica, and, yes, the woman was as innocent as she looked. No skeletons in her closet. Just a desperate woman looking for her brother. *A woman who is about to trust the wrong man.*

Outside he saw Veronica hop into a small blue sedan. Nothing fancy or particularly noticeable about it. Her taillights flashed on, and she quickly reversed.

Then she pulled away from Last Chance.

He watched her, his gaze lingering and…

Another pair of headlights flashed on in the parking lot. His gaze shot to the right just as a vehicle's motor growled and a car lurched forward. When it reached the parking lot's exit, the vehicle turned to the left and headed in the same direction that Veronica had just taken.

*Just another bar patron, leaving for the night.*

Only Jasper hadn't seen anyone get in that vehicle. So the driver had been sitting inside for a while, doing what? Talking on his phone? Yeah, maybe.

*Waiting for Veronica?*

That made no sense. So the driver had taken the same road that Veronica had taken.

It didn't mean anything, despite the kick in his gut.

He was seeing danger where there was none. A definite downside of his job. After so many missions, so many deaths, he saw danger everywhere.

Jasper turned back toward Last Chance.

Sometimes a car was just a car.

He looked over his shoulder at the darkness, unable to shake the tension that had tightened his body. *Because sometimes danger could really be anyplace.*

SHE HAD THE radio blaring. The loud music helped to keep Veronica's mind off the fact that it was after midnight and she was on one long, lonely stretch of Texas road.

There were no streetlights. Streetlights weren't exactly a priority on this seldom-traveled highway.

Darkness surrounded her, a pitch-black night cut only by the flash of her headlights.

The music kept blaring, and she gripped the steering wheel tightly. Thirty more minutes, and she'd turn off this road and head back toward the ranch.

She'd done it. She'd gotten Jasper to help her and—

Bright lights suddenly filled her rearview mirror. The whole interior of her car lit up, and her eyes had to squint against that strong glare.

*Guess I'm not alone anymore.*

The other vehicle came up behind her, driving fast. Going far faster than she was.

Veronica eased her foot off the gas. If the other vehicle wanted to pass her, that was fine. She wasn't about to try to race anyone in the dark.

The vehicle came closer and closer, eating up the miles between them. It was hard to tell what kind of car was behind her. The driver had on his bright lights, too, and that vehicle was right on her tail now.

She lifted her hand, waving vaguely to indicate that the other vehicle should pass her.

A motor revved behind her. Then the other car shot into the left lane. Her breath eased out and she slowed down even more. He was going to pass her. Good. That was—

The other vehicle was right beside her. Only the driver wasn't going so fast now. He'd lowered his speed to match hers.

A shiver slid over her, and Veronica glanced over at the other vehicle. She couldn't see anyone inside. Too dark. She just had the impression of a long, heavy car.

The other car seemed to be coming closer to her. *Coming closer—*

She slammed on her brakes.

The other car kept going.

Her breath eased out even as her heart pounded frantically in her chest. For a moment there, she'd remembered another wreck, a time that had destroyed her life. Her eyes squeezed shut. *"You're safe. Everything's okay."* Cale had told her those words, over and over again as he comforted her through the nightmares that had seeped into her life when she'd been a child.

She wasn't a child now. Her eyes opened. She stared straight ahead.

Then she saw the red flash of the other car's taillights. After that brief stop, the vehicle spun around and came right toward her. The motor was snarling.

She shoved her foot down on the gas and tried to swerve around that vehicle, but the driver anticipated her move. His car lunged toward hers. Veronica screamed and yanked the steering wheel to the left.

Her car narrowly missed the other vehicle, but her little sedan careened off the road, bounced and slammed into a wooden fence. She flew forward, her head snapping down, even as the seat belt bit into her shoulder and yanked her back in place.

*Holding her prisoner, trapping her...just like before.*

Her air bag deployed, sending a white cloud all around her, and she fought against it, pushing with her fists and calling out for help.

Someone yanked open her passenger's-side door. *Help?*

"Get her!" a voice barked. "Hurry the hell up!"

The air bag deflated instantly—because someone had just shoved a knife into it. The gleaming blade of the knife shone in the darkness.

Then that blade came toward her. Veronica screamed.

But who was out there to hear her cries? She was in the middle of nowhere, and the man with the knife wasn't hesitating as he jerked her out of the car.

## Chapter Two

It was a scene out of a nightmare.

Jasper slammed on the brakes when he rounded the corner and saw the crashed sedan. The front of the vehicle was lodged in a fence, and the driver's-side door was hanging open.

His gaze shot back across the two-lane highway. The other car—the bigger vehicle—was parked sideways, cutting across the pavement, and its doors were open, too.

Jasper jumped out of his truck.

Two men were trying to shove something—*some-one*—into the trunk of that gray car. Veronica? *Hell, no.*

He had his weapon out in less than a second's time. "Let her go!" he roared even as he raced toward the men.

A swear broke from one of the men. They dumped Veronica into the trunk. One guy tried to slam the lid shut on her.

"I *will* shoot you! Get away from her!"

Veronica tried to jump out of the trunk. One of the thugs shoved her back inside.

*I warned you.*

Jasper aimed at the man who'd pushed Veronica. Fired. The bullet tore into her attacker's shoulder, and he stumbled back, screaming. The other man rushed toward the driver's side. He dived into the vehicle even as Veronica leaped out of the trunk. She started running toward Jasper as the driver rushed away with a screech of burning rubber.

The driver *thought* he was getting away. Just leaving his bleeding buddy behind. *Think again.* "Get down, Veronica!" Jasper shouted.

She instantly hit the pavement. He fired. Once. Twice. The bullets found their targets as he aimed at back tires. The vehicle was still lurching forward, but the driver wasn't getting far, not on those tires. Jasper yanked out his phone. He had Gunner on the line in less than five seconds. "Got a fleeing vehicle on 59, back tires are out."

That was all he'd need to say. Gunner would stop the driver. If not Gunner, then one of the other agents in the area. The EOD always had his back.

Jasper kept his weapon out as he hurried toward Veronica. The gray car had disappeared around the curve, but Jasper knew he'd be seeing that guy again real soon. But right now, Veronica was his priority.

She was still lying flat on the ground. "Is it...okay to move?" she called out, voice trembling.

He glanced at the man he'd shot. The guy had slammed his head into the back of the car when he fell, and it looked as though the would-be kidnapper was now out cold. But Jasper wasn't taking any chances. "Get up, but stay with me."

She pushed to her feet. In the darkness, he couldn't tell much about her or any injuries she might have. "Did they hurt you?"

Veronica shook her head. "They were— They tried to kidnap me!"

Which didn't make a hell of a lot of sense to him.

He headed toward the downed man. Veronica's hesitant steps followed him. His shot had been clean, right in and out of the shoulder. Jasper felt for the guy's pulse. Found the steady beat. He searched the guy, taking away a very sharp knife from the sheath on the man's hip.

*Just what did you plan to do with this?*

Another car rushed past them. Gunner. And Jasper could hear yet another vehicle coming from the north, heading in to cut off their escaping kidnapper.

No one was getting away.

He risked a fast glance back at Veronica. Her shoulders were hunched. Her arms were wrapped around her stomach, as if she were hugging herself.

"Did they say anything to you?"

She hesitated, then shook her head.

Just what was up with that hesitation?

Her gaze was on his gun.

The weapon might be making her nervous, but now wasn't the time to be putting the weapon up. He'd keep his weapon at the ready until the scene was secure.

He just hated the way Veronica looked. Shaken. Scared. "You're safe." His words were gruff.

Her chin jerked up. Then she gave a slow nod.

That wasn't good enough for him. Damn if he didn't find himself going closer to her. Pulling her against him. Holding her with one arm while his other kept his gun aimed at the unconscious man on the ground. "I won't let anyone hurt you," he told Veronica. He took a breath and caught the sweet scent rising from her hair. Honeysuckle. A scent that he remembered from what seemed like a lifetime ago.

Her arms curled around his waist. "I thought they were going to kill me."

They just might have. If he hadn't followed his instincts and followed *her*.

But he'd been in too many tight situations to just ignore the battle-ready tension that served to heighten his senses when danger was near.

Jasper stared down at Veronica. She'd lost her shoes, and the top of her head barely reached his chin. He wasn't sure what was happening—some sick punks who'd tried to abduct a pretty woman out on her own or…

*Was this about Cale?*

The faint wail of a siren sounded in the distance.

Jasper tensed. Who'd called the cops? Not his team; they wouldn't alert anyone local. They liked to handle their business in-house.

And Veronica didn't exactly have a phone in her hands or *wait*... His eyes narrowed

Yes, she did have a phone clutched in her fingers.

He felt the small ridge of her phone pressing against his side. "Veronica, did you call for help?"

She nodded. "I texted the sheriff. He didn't believe me about Cale, but Wyatt was supposed to be patrolling around here tonight. I thought he could help me."

He could. The cavalry was flying in toward them. Jasper knew that he had just a few minutes with Veronica before the sheriff arrived.

So he had to set up his cover and he had to do it fast. "He'll wonder why we're out here. And I'm guessing Last Chance isn't your usual kind of hang-out spot."

She shook her head.

"Don't tell him you just hired yourself a mercenary." He didn't want the sheriff getting in his way. In fact, the EOD would have to take steps to move him *out* of their way. "Tell him we're together. I'm an old friend."

"A friend of Cale's," she whispered.

"Right." The attempted kidnapping had just changed his plans. *I have to stay close to her.* "If he asks, tell the sheriff that I'm staying at the ranch with you."

"I don't know…" Veronica began as she tried to ease away from him.

Jasper just held her tighter. "After what just happened, do you really want to go back to the ranch alone tonight?"

"No."

Good answer. Because he wasn't in the mood to force his way inside the ranch, but if he had to do it, he would. Paired with Cale's disappearance, the kidnapping was just too much of a coincidence for him to handle.

He'd never liked coincidences.

But since he had her agreement, Jasper eased his hold on Veronica. Only she didn't step back.

"Thank you," she told him.

The words were soft. Whispered from between her lips.

Lips that he was suddenly way too aware of in that moment. His heart was racing, his muscles locked and tight as adrenaline burned through him.

"Thank you for saving me."

He didn't want her thanks, but Jasper was uncomfortably aware that he wanted *her*. Since that first look in the bar, he'd wanted her, wanted the one woman he was about to betray.

Fate always enjoyed playing her games with him.

He offered Veronica a smile and hoped the darkness hid the intensity of his eyes. "Hey, you'd already called the sheriff." A sheriff who was coming closer and closer with each passing moment. "Seems like you were doing a fine job of saving yourself."

The scream of the siren was nearly upon them. The flashing lights from the sheriff's car illuminated the scene. The fact that Jasper was holding a weapon meant he could expect a loud—

Brakes squealed. The sheriff jumped from his car and yelled, "Drop your weapon! Get away from the woman!"

Only the woman in question wasn't exactly trying to get away from him. Veronica positioned her body in front of Jasper's. "He saved me! Wyatt, stop! Jasper isn't the bad guy!"

Oh, if she only knew.

But Jasper knew how to play the game. He dropped his weapon, one of his weapons, anyway, and put his hands up.

"Two men tried to kidnap me!" Veronica rushed to explain. "This guy over here…" She jerked her thumb to the man on the ground. "And another guy. They forced me off the road. Jasper stopped them before they could drive away with me!"

"Another guy?" the sheriff repeated. Jasper couldn't tell much about the man; he was behind the lights, and his body was covered by the darkness. "What guy?"

"*This* guy," came Gunner's familiar voice as he

walked out of the darkness. The perp was in front of him, taking slow, sullen steps.

The sheriff swore and jerked his gun toward Gunner. This was probably as much excitement he'd ever seen out on that highway. Pulling over drunks versus catching kidnappers.

Yeah, the normal routine had just been blown away.

"Easy," Gunner said to the sheriff, voice deadly soft. "I've got the man subdued."

The perp's hands were behind his back, and Jasper had no doubt they were cuffed.

"Who are you?" the sheriff demanded, his gaze locked on Gunner—or what he could see of Gunner.

"I'm a federal agent," Gunner said, flashing his ID very, very fast. Mostly because it wasn't legit. Sure, they were federal agents, but they didn't exactly carry around ID that would ever tie them back to the EOD.

"You an agent, too?" the sheriff asked as he swung his attention back to Jasper.

"No, he's a friend of mine," Veronica said before Jasper could respond. It was a good thing that she was so quick to reply. It saved Jasper from having to tell a lie in front of her.

The sheriff began to slowly lower his gun. "I don't understand. I was just patrolling a few miles away... What the hell is going on here?"

"That's what I'd like to know." Jasper glanced at

Gunner's prisoner. The man's body was stiff, angry. Did the guy think he was tough?

Jasper had broken plenty of tough targets in his time.

This guy would fall, too, and Jasper would find out just why the men had been after Veronica.

IT WASN'T HER first time at the small sheriff's station in Whiskey Ridge, Texas. But it was the first time that she'd been afraid of the men who stood in the nine-by-twelve-foot cell.

Veronica edged back, deliberately placing her body close to Jasper's. He was talking to his buddy, the guy who was some kind of federal agent. The man—Gunner something—said that he'd been on his way to meet Jasper for a drink when he got the call about the attack on the road.

Wyatt was pacing nervously in front of the prisoners. His hair, short and black, jutted out at odd angles, the result of him running desperate fingers over his head. He kept casting worried looks at Veronica every few minutes, and he'd already asked at least a dozen times, "Sure you're all right?"

Other than a few bruises, she was fine.

Things could have been much worse, and she knew it.

"You got a permit for that weapon?" Wyatt demanded of Jasper. Wyatt's dark eyes had narrowed.

Jasper nodded.

Veronica's hands fisted. "I don't think that's the priority here." She knew Wyatt was a by-the-book guy, but didn't an attempted kidnapping trump a weapons charge?

Wyatt flushed, but held his ground. "Those guys aren't talking." His thumb jerked over his shoulder toward the cell. "Not a damn word. I'm running their prints, so we should at least know who the hell they are soon."

She risked a look at the men and found them both glaring at her. The town's doc had come in and patched up the injured man. The bullet had gone straight through his shoulder. Easy in and out. But the concussion he'd received when his head slammed into the trunk had him dazed.

"Those were some damn fine shots," Wyatt said, but the words weren't a compliment. They reeked of suspicion. "One blast to the shoulder, two shots that both hit the tires of a moving vehicle."

"The vehicle wasn't exactly moving fast," Jasper murmured. "The driver was just pulling off when I made the hits."

She just remembered the smell of burnt rubber. The squeal of tires. The thunder of the shots. Veronica cut her gaze back to the sheriff.

Wyatt was frowning. His face wasn't as hard as Jasper's. His features were softer, rounder, with a few more lines around the eyes. He was good-looking, when he wasn't sweating bullets—which he was doing right then.

But despite his sweat and tension, Wyatt's stare was knowing as it lingered on Jasper. "You're real comfortable with a gun."

She didn't like where this was going. "That's because he's a former army ranger. He served in the military with…with Cale."

That revelation had both of Wyatt's brows rising. "Did he now."

That news had just led to even more suspicion in his gaze. Not what she'd wanted to happen. "I was just… I'd been going through some old photographs of Cale's recently, hoping to find something that might help me locate him." That was one hundred percent true. She'd dug out every photograph she could find, desperate for any clue, no matter how small. "I saw Jasper in some of the photos, and I remembered how close he and Jasper used to be." Again, all true. She'd seen Jasper's photograph, remembered just how deadly Cale had said that the ex-ranger had been, and she'd known that she needed a man like Jasper to help her. A bit of checking on her computer, and she'd realized fate was on her side.

Jasper had been in the area.

"So she called me up," Jasper said, interrupting easily and just taking up the story now. "We got to talking, I came here…" His fingers slid down her arm. "One thing led to another. I'm sure you know how that can be."

Wyatt's jaw locked. "But what brought you out on that road tonight? When you were supposed to meet your friend at Last Chance?"

There wasn't a whole lot of privacy to be found in the sheriff's station, but they'd moved far enough away from the prisoners so that the jailed men couldn't hear their quiet words. Veronica was glad to be away from those men. The intensity of their stares unnerved her. *They tried to kidnap me.*

She'd never come that close to violence like that before. Never had violence actually directed *at* her. Cale had always protected her from everything and everyone.

Cale wasn't there anymore.

"Even though my friend was coming, I didn't want Veronica driving home alone. I figured Gunner could wait a bit." Jasper reached for her hand. Shocked her when he lifted her fingers to his mouth and brushed a light kiss over her knuckles. "So I followed her, and I'm damn glad that I did."

Her heart had slammed into her chest. *I'm glad, too.*

"I want to talk with these prisoners," Gunner suddenly said. *"Alone."*

Wyatt tensed, then glanced over at the deputy who was on duty that night, a young guy with pale skin and wide eyes. She knew the deputy well, as well as she knew Wyatt. Deputy Jimmy Jones had lived in Whiskey Ridge his whole life. Quiet, shy, but the twenty-two-year-old was fierce about protecting those in his county.

When she'd first met Jimmy, she'd felt much sympathy for him because the boy he'd been...well, his life had been a nightmare. But Jimmy had pulled himself out of that darkness, and now he was fighting to be better, stronger.

"Why are you wanting to talk to *my* prisoners without me present?" Wyatt asked. "That's not what I'd call regular—"

Gunner lifted out his ID again. "I want to talk to them because I think they might fit it on *my* case." A brief pause, then, "They fit the profile of some men I've been tracking with the FBI."

They did? That was news to Veronica.

Jasper's fingers tightened around hers.

"Let me talk to them and see if we need to take over jurisdiction here." Gunner shrugged and walked toward the glaring men in the cell. "If I can tie them to the other abductions..." He said this part loudly, deliberately so, or at least that was what Veronica thought.

The injured man, a wiry guy with light blue eyes and sandy hair, seemed to pale even more. Then, for the first time, he spoke, shouting, "We didn't take anyone!"

"Anyone else, you mean," Gunner corrected. Then

he glanced over his shoulder at Wyatt. "Give me some time with them, alone. I'll find out everything I need to know in my interrogation."

Jasper nodded, as if granting his permission. Veronica frowned, but Jasper said, "You take care of them, Gunner, and I'll take Veronica home."

*Home?*

But Wyatt was nodding now, too. Well, wasn't it great that they were all in agreement? She was breaking apart on the inside, and they'd formed some sort of guys' club.

"You do need to head home, Veronica," Wyatt told her. "We'll take care of these men."

She didn't move. Her gaze had turned back to the two men. Their faces were now etched in her memory. They were young, younger than she'd suspected when their car had first slammed into hers. They barely looked twenty. One still had acne.

And they were sweating. More so than Wyatt. They looked afraid and as she swept a fast glance at the man called Gunner, she realized that they *should* be afraid.

Jasper was danger wrapped up in a handsome package. Gunner...he was just lethal. An icy intensity burned in his dark eyes, and his hard features hinted at the hell he must have seen over the years. This was a man well acquainted with death and darkness. This was a man who scared her.

Her breath eased out slowly. Despite the fact that

both Jasper and Wyatt wanted her to head home, Veronica wanted to stay. She wanted to face these men and find out just why they'd tried to take her.

*"You can't hide from the dark."* Another rule from her brother. *"The night comes whether you want it to or not."* He'd first spouted that one when she was seven and terrified of monsters. She'd wanted to hide in her closet.

Now she knew that hiding did no good. The monsters, the real ones, could find you no matter where you went.

She took a deep breath and headed toward that cell. Jasper tensed and gritted, *"Veronica."*

She kept walking and only stopped when she was a foot away from the bars. "Why?"

The injured man flinched.

"Why did you hit my car? Why did you try to take me?" They'd both had knives. Both had threatened her with them, but the blades had never sliced her skin.

Wyatt grabbed her arm. "You can't do this."

Um, she *was* doing this. Because she wasn't a coward. These men wouldn't make her cower in the dark. *The night comes...*

Wyatt tried to pull her toward him. "There are rules about questioning suspects. They have rights. You can't just—"

"I have rights, too," she snapped back at him as a sharp burst of anger filled her chest, driving right past the chilling fear that she'd known for the past few hours. "I think I have the right not to be stuffed in the back of a trunk on a Saturday night."

"She does have that right," Gunner murmured.

Her gaze cut to his. It almost looked as if he was about to smile.

"Do you want these bozos getting released on some technicality that a lawyer tosses up at us? Some B.S. about them not having counsel?" Wyatt's tension had doubled.

As far as she knew, the men hadn't asked for lawyers. They hadn't asked for anything.

"I've got this," Wyatt told her, voice deepening. "Let me do my job, okay? Trust me."

But he hadn't done his job before. When her brother had vanished, he'd done nothing.

She pulled away from him, stared once more at the men. Jasper wasn't saying anything. He'd just come up to stand behind her. Silent. Strong.

When her brother hadn't come back after a few weeks, she'd started digging. Pushing. Pushing as hard as she could as she dug into his life and the faint trail that he'd left behind.

Had someone tried to push back?

"Is this about Cale?" she asked softly.

She saw the injured man's eyelids flicker.

Her heart seemed to stop. Then it raced, faster and faster with each second that ticked by. "Do you know where he is?" Veronica demanded, and she lunged for the bars.

Jasper grabbed her, wrapping his arms around her stomach and hauling her back against him.

The men in the cell were smirking now. The taller one, the one with dark brown hair, took a step toward her. "Don't know your brother."

Jasper's hands squeezed her tighter.

Through numb lips, she managed to say, "I never said Cale was my brother."

That made the smirk vanish. The guy's eyes cut to Wyatt and blazed a wild blue. "We want a lawyer, *now.*"

"Tell me about my brother!" Veronica yelled back.

Jasper pulled her even closer against him. She could feel the rock-hard muscles of his abs against her back. His head lowered. "Easy," he whispered in her ear.

Did it look as if she could take this easy? The guy had just admitted to knowing her brother. Random abduction? No way. No. Way.

Wyatt slammed his hand against the bars. *"Veronica."*

Jasper growled. "Watch that tone, Sheriff."

Wyatt shoved both of his hands into his hair. "They asked for a lawyer. We have to get them one." He pointed to the deputy. "Go get Tanner Dempsey. He still occasionally practices some defense over in Dallas."

As far as Veronica knew, Tanner Dempsey was the only lawyer within a two-hundred-mile radius. She'd thought he gave up law after he'd lost that last big case in Dallas, but maybe anyone with a law license would do right now.

When Jimmy rushed to the back of the station, and the back exit, Wyatt glanced at Veronica. Heaving a sigh, the sheriff waved toward his office. "Go cool down in there. When Tanner gets here—"

"It's the middle of the night," Veronica said, shaking her head. "There's no telling how long it will take Tanner to get here." Provided he was even in town.

A muscle flexed in Wyatt's jaw. "They aren't going anywhere," he gritted. "And if you don't want to go home, then at least get in my office. You *can't* be near these prisoners."

Now she was the one to glare at the men in that cell.

"Don't worry," Gunner's rumbling voice promised, "I'll find out exactly why these men tried to abduct you."

Of course, she wanted to know why the men had targeted her, but right now her priority was finding Cale. "I just want my brother back."

"This is a lead," Jasper whispered in her ear. "Settle down. We can make this work for us."

Settling down wasn't exactly easy. Not after everything that had happened.

He led her toward the sheriff's office. As they walked away, she saw Gunner taking out his phone and heading for the station's front doors. "Where's he going?" she asked. The prisoners were the other way. He wasn't going to find out much by heading outside.

"He'll be checking in with his superiors. Briefing them on what's happening."

Oh, right. Gunner had said that he was already working some abductions in the area.

Jasper shut the door behind them and exhaled on a hard breath. She rubbed her arms, feeling chilled as the air blew down on her from the vent overhead.

His finger rose and traced over her arms, making goose bumps. "Are you sure you're all right?"

She nodded. She couldn't hear any sounds from the outer area. The blinds were all shut in Wyatt's office, effectively closing them off and giving them a bit of privacy.

"When I saw the crash and those guys trying to stuff you in that trunk…" His hand fell away from her. "You scared me."

She blinked at his words, taken aback. "*I* scared you? I didn't think anything could scare someone like you."

He stared at her intently, like a snake targeting his prey. "A guy like me?"

She'd said the wrong thing. She was nervous and scared and when he was this close, she just felt hyperaware of him. Veronica shifted from one high heel to the other. She really hated these shoes. "You know what you are. You've seen so much. Done so much. You've—"

"Killed?"

There it was. He'd just tossed it right out. So she wouldn't back down. "Yes."

His pupils seemed to expand, the darkness taking over the green of his eyes. "Every man can know fear, but you can't ever let that fear stop you."

Sounded as though he had his own set of rules to follow.

"I said I'd help you." He took a step forward. She refused to retreat. So he just got...very close to her. Her breath came a little faster. Her mouth seemed to go dry. Especially when he added, "But my help has conditions."

"Conditions?" She had to tilt her head back to better meet his gaze.

"You hired me to find your brother, but you didn't say anything about your own life being at risk."

"Th-that's because I didn't think I was at risk." And, dang it all, her stutter had come back. She'd tried so hard to defeat that stutter over the years, but when she got too nervous, it still slipped out. Being around Jasper, yes, he made her *too nervous*.

"Someone just tried to abduct you. I'd say that definitely puts you in the 'at risk' category."

She tried to get him back on track. "They know my brother."

He nodded. "Yes."

"They're a lead for us!"

Another nod.

She wasn't sure where this was going, so Veronica just asked, "Are you... Do you not want to help me anymore because of the attack?" While she waited on his response, she pretty much held her breath. *Don't back away, don't back away, don't—*

The faint lines around his eyes deepened. "I don't back off a job, no matter what. You should remember that."

Um, okay. She would. She tended to have a very good memory.

"The fact that you seem to be in danger, that means that I'm gonna be staying close to you, real close."

He was already close. So close that she could feel the heat of his body against hers.

"I'll find Cale, but I'm not going to risk you in the process."

A mercenary with a heart? She wasn't surprised. Cale had a good heart, too, despite what the rest of the world seemed to think.

"Will you trust me?" Jasper asked her.

She nodded. At this point, he was the only one she could trust. No one else had been willing to help her. Only Jasper.

His pupils had definitely gotten bigger. They almost swallowed the green of his eyes. "Good." Then his fingers were under her chin. His head was bending toward her.

Was he…was he about to kiss her?

Veronica was pretty sure she'd had this dream once, only she hadn't been recovering from a near kidnapping in the dream.

"I won't let you get hurt," he promised. His voice was rough and dark, the way that she thought it would sound when he was in bed with a woman, whispering in the night.

Her gaze fell to his mouth.

She wanted him to kiss her.

She arched toward him. Maybe she even rose onto her tiptoes.

He wasn't closing the distance between them.

*I want to kiss him.* Maybe it was the adrenaline and the fear still pumping through her. Whatever it was, in that one instant, Veronica felt a little bit wild.

Wild enough to curl her hands around his shoulders. To pull him down against her and to press her lips against his. His lips were firm and a little cool. And they were opening beneath hers. She'd initiated the kiss, but Jasper quickly took over. His lips hardened on hers, and his tongue swept inside her mouth, sliding right past her lips. He didn't rush the kiss. Didn't try to take too much from her, too fast.

He explored. He tasted. He made her knees feel a little bit weak, and he made her smell smoke.

Smell…smoke?

Jasper pulled his head away from hers. "What the hell?"

He whirled away and yanked open the office door. Over his shoulder, Veronica caught a glimpse of Wyatt rushing toward them.

"Get out of here!" Wyatt yelled. He had keys in his hand. "The storage room in the back is burning!"

Then Veronica heard the crackles of flames.

An explosion shook the building, reverberating with a stunning echo even as a blast of heat seemed to lance over her skin.

Before she could do more than suck in a shocked breath, Jasper was hauling her out of the office and away from the flames—flames that weren't just in the back room any longer. The flames were spreading around the station, burning with deadly ferocity.

*Burning.*

Everything around them was burning as greedy flames leaped across the station, destroying everything in their path.

# Chapter Three

"Keep her safe," Jasper barked as he pushed Veronica toward Gunner. The sniper had just come back through the station's front door, rushing toward the flames, and his timing was pretty damn perfect. Jasper wanted a guard on Veronica while he went back in to help the sheriff, and Gunner was one of the best guards that Jasper had ever met.

Gunner nodded, but his gaze drifted back to the flames. Jasper knew that Gunner wanted to be the one running back inside. The guy was always drawn to the fire.

One of his good points.

And his weaknesses.

"Jasper!" Veronica called his name as he ran back inside. He didn't stop. Wyatt would need another pair of hands to get those prisoners out of that burning building.

The fire wasn't one that would be controlled easily. He'd heard that explosion, a too-familiar sound. The initial flames in the storage room had been a

diversion. The detonation he'd heard had been deliberate. A trap.

A premeditated inferno.

Once he made it back to the holding area, Jasper saw that Wyatt had his gun on the prisoners.
He'd already cuffed them and was trying to lead
them outside. He couldn't do the job alone. Jasper
grabbed the first guy, then ducked low to try to get
some fresh air into his lungs. "Get your butt out of
here!" he ordered the guy.

Wyatt whirled on him. "The deputy...Jimmy...
he came back... I've got to find him..."

Jasper nodded grimly. "I've got these two." The
would-be kidnappers were shaking with their fear.
They just wanted to get away from the fire. They
weren't planning an attack on him.

The sheriff coughed. He started to hand Jasper
his gun, then hesitated.

"There's a federal agent..." Jasper covered his
mouth. The flames were getting worse. The sprin-
klers had shot on overhead, but they weren't doing
much of a job at stopping the flames. "The agent's
right outside." *And one is right in front of you.* "You
can count on us."

The sheriff gave him the gun.

Jasper led out the two prisoners. He cast one quick
look back at the sheriff. He sure hoped that Wyatt
knew what he was doing. Jasper didn't like leaving

any man to the flames. Leaving a man behind—
that wasn't the way he was programmed to operate.

The prisoners rushed outside. And, as he'd expected, Gunner was there, waiting on them. Gunner
had his gun drawn and a fierce *don't try anything*
expression etched on his face.

Jasper glanced back at the station's door. Where
was the sheriff? Would he come out the front or
make his way out the back?

He'd go check, make sure everyone was safe and—

Gunfire ripped through the night. One blast. Two.

The two prisoners fell instantly. Blood bloomed
on their chests and their bodies hit the pavement.

Swearing, Jasper leaped forward and slammed his
body into Veronica's. They fell to the ground, and
he kept her covered, using his body as a shield. At
any moment, he expected to hear the blast of more
gunfire, and he expected to feel bullets slam into
his back. *"Gunner!"* Jasper bellowed. His yell was
an order. Jasper would protect Veronica, and Gunner would find the shooter.

Keeping his body over Veronica's, Jasper led her
behind his parked truck. It wasn't much in the way
of shelter, but it was better than nothing. An old garage was at their back, the truck in front of them.

Jasper's head turned toward the men on the
ground. They weren't moving, and that dark bloom
on their chests told him that he wouldn't be getting
any more information from them.

Heart shots. Both of them. Dead-on. Just...

*Dead.*

Veronica was silent beneath him. He heard foot-steps pounding toward him and he looked up to see an ash-covered Wyatt racing across the station's small parking lot. The deputy—pale, with wide eyes—was right on his heels. The men were right out in the open. Perfect targets.

"Get down!" Jasper roared at them. "We've got a shooter." A very skilled shooter who'd just taken out two men who were less than five feet away from Jasper.

Two men...but after those hits, the gunman hadn't fired another shot. Gunner and Veronica were the two who'd been out in the open the longest.

*He didn't aim for us.* He'd waited and taken the shots when his real targets came out of the sheriff's station.

"Stay low," Jasper ordered Veronica as he finally lifted his body off hers. "Keep your head down," he told her because the last thing he wanted was for her to become a target.

She grabbed his hand when he turned to leave. "Where are you going?" There was a scratch on her cheek, and her palms looked red and raw. Jasper knew the injuries had come from the impact, when he'd shoved her to the ground.

Just for a second, his fingers brushed over the

scrapes on her palm. Then he told her the truth, "I'm going hunting." Because that was what he did best.

Her face tensed, but he didn't hesitate any longer. He got his weapon ready and eased away from his cover. He knew where the gunfire had come from. He'd been trained to track back to the source of a shot. In the dead of night like this, no one else was around, so the tracking was even easier for him. A fast glance assured him that the little strip in town was deserted. Flames kept crackling, and Jasper didn't even know where the fire department was, but he sure hoped Wyatt was calling for help.

Moving with barely a whisper of sound, Jasper headed up to the right. He caught a glimpse of Gunner, moving fast in the same direction. They were both closing in on their prey. The angle of the shots, the trajectory—they knew where their shooter should be.

Only when they closed in, he wasn't there. No one was there.

Jasper spun around, searching the darkness. Damn it. A car or motorcycle could have crept quietly away, its movements easily covered by the crackle of the flames. If the shooter had escaped in a vehicle, they wouldn't be able to tell for sure in the darkness. When morning came, they'd be able to check in the light. Look for tracks in the dirt roads and gravel and—

Thunder rumbled, and it was definitely thunder this time, not another gunshot.

His teeth snapped together. Rain would destroy any tracks. Hell, hell, *hell.* The shooter was about to have one lucky getaway.

"Are we clear?" That had to be the deputy's voice. Cutting high with fear and trembling in the night. "Is it safe to come out?"

Jasper and Gunner shared a long look. They might be clear, for the moment, but the killer had just sent them one blunt message.

*I'm here. I'm watching.*

*I'm killing.*

The shooter had just executed two men right in front of EOD agents. The guy wasn't playing.

That was fine, because Jasper wasn't playing, He would find the killer. Find him. Stop him. Permanently.

The flames were still raging. Jasper tucked the gun in the back of his jeans. He needed to find some water, some hoses. Do whatever he could to stop that fire until backup arrived.

He returned to the bodies and found Wyatt crouched over the men. The sheriff gave a sad shake of his head as he felt for a pulse along the necks of the fallen men.

*The backup will be too late.* No EMTs would be able to save these guys.

Someone hadn't wanted the men to talk. So now they'd never say another word to anyone.

THE STORM HIT just before dawn, rushing in with heavy rain and strong winds. The weather forecaster had warned that they'd be in for some hard weather for the next week.

No one had warned that death would be coming, too.

Veronica opened the door to the main ranch house. The lights flickered on instantly, part of the security system that Cale had installed. The alarm began to beep, signaling that the door had been opened. Jasper followed behind her, shaking his booted heels, then heading inside the foyer.

The big house seemed smaller the instant he entered.

She hurried forward and reset the alarm. "We should…um… You can have the room at the top of the stairs." She waved her hand vaguely toward the staircase. "It's Cale's room, and since he's not here…"

*Where are you, Cale?*

"…he won't mind you using it," she finished quietly.

Jasper nodded and just kept watching her with that too-intense stare. She almost felt as if his stare saw right through her, to the insecure girl she kept holed up inside.

"I—I'm going to shower." She *hated* that stutter. For the most part, she could control it, but when Jasper turned that laserlike gaze of his on her, she got too nervous. Veronica turned away from him, determined to keep her composure. At least for a little while longer. Those men were dead. Shot, right in front of her. She'd seen the injured man's face when the bullet hit him. The horror. The flash of pain. Then...the mask of death. Veronica rubbed her chilled arms and told Jasper, "The kitchen's down the hallway. You can help yourself to—"

"That's it?"

Veronica glanced back at him. He was stalking toward her. Looking sexy and dangerous with a faint line of stubble coating his jaw. "You seen a lot of death, Veronica Lane?" Jasper asked in that deep, rumbling voice of his.

Not a lot. Some. More than she wanted to see. Wasn't that the way it was for people?

"Because when most folks see two men get shot to death in front of them, they don't turn to ice."

They did if the ice was the only thing that could protect them.

"Make me understand you." His voice was gruff now. And there it was. He was looking at her as if she was *off,* different. Story of her life. Everyone but Cale had always thought she was different. Too quiet. Too shy. Too...well, everything.

Forcing her spine to straighten, Veronica held Jasper's gaze. She didn't owe him any explanations. He'd been hired to do a job, simple as that. She didn't divulge her personal history to anyone because it was *personal.*

But he'd put his body over hers. Covered her and been willing to take a bullet to keep her safe. She remembered the feel of his body against hers. Strong muscles, hard flesh. His breath had whispered near her ear. He'd held her tight, shielding her from the gunfire.

Jasper risking his life in order to keep her safe— that hadn't exactly been covered in their one-thousand-dollar-a-day deal that had been brokered before she'd left Last Chance.

So, maybe, *definitely,* she did owe the guy some kind of explanation. She'd bare her soul to him, as she hadn't done to anyone else.

"I've seen dead bodies before." She pressed her lips together. This wasn't a memory she enjoyed visiting. "My parents died in a car accident when I was six."

"Cale mentioned—"

"I was in the backseat." Her words tumbled over his because she wanted to get this story out as quickly as she could. If she said it fast, then maybe she wouldn't have to think about it too long. Maybe it wouldn't hurt so much. "We were on our way to pick up Cale from his soccer game." As soon as the car had stopped rolling, the silence had hit her. Then she'd screamed. She'd known something was wrong with her mother right away. She'd called for her, but her mother hadn't answered.

Her dad had. His voice had been weak as he'd told her, *"Don't cry, baby. Don't cry."*

She hadn't been able to stop. She'd cried and cried—especially when her dad had stopped talking to her.

"The other driver was drunk. He was knocked unconscious when the cars hit and he... It took him a while to wake up." And to make his way to her car. To find the screaming child trapped in the back.

Jasper's arms were around her. He hauled her close. She could feel the rapid beating of his heart against her. "I'm sorry."

So was she.

"I didn't know you were— Cale never mentioned you were *in* the car."

Because Cale liked to pretend that she hadn't been. Or that she didn't remember. That she'd never seen blood and death. That she hadn't known fear.

That all the years in foster care hadn't existed for either of them.

But you couldn't just wipe away the past.

She forced herself to step back from Jasper even though the warmth of his arms was so tempting. "So I've seen death before, but...but I wasn't ready for what I saw tonight." Who could be? She saw again the horror in that man's eyes. The pain. Then...*noth-*

*ing.* "The fact that I don't break down, it doesn't mean I don't care."

"It just means you're strong," he said.

Strong? Not many people had called her that before. Cale was the strong one. She was the smart one. At least, those were the tags they'd been given in foster care. But she'd told him enough about herself for now, and he wasn't trying to break through the ice that shielded her any longer. She swallowed and tried to focus less on death. *I don't want to keep seeing that man's eyes go blank.* "That special agent... Gunner..." The man who'd stayed behind at the scene while Jasper took her home. "How do you two know each other?" She'd been distracted before, hadn't even really processed that an FBI agent had appeared at her kidnapping scene. Talk about some luck. She'd known that Jasper had connections she could use; she just hadn't expected to use those connections instantly.

"I do some freelance work for the government." His answer came easily. His gaze held hers. "Gunner and I have worked together on missions in the past."

The words held the ring of truth, but then, why would she even think that he'd lie to her? So far, he'd done nothing but save her. "He'll tell you what he finds out about those men?"

Jasper nodded.

"Why do you think they were shot?" She was exhausted. Her body hurt. But she couldn't stop talking. The questions she was asking him…part of the reason why she was bringing them up was that she wanted to steer him away from her parents. Her past. That wound was still raw.

"They're dead because someone wanted to make sure they didn't talk."

She thought so, too. "About Cale?"

He didn't answer. Maybe that was answer enough. Bracing herself, she asked, "Do you think my brother is dead?" Had he been shot like those two men, gunned down with no warning? No time to fight or plead or live?

He took a step away from her. "I absolutely think Cale is alive."

Finally, she could pull in a deep breath.

"I swear to you, I *will* find him."

She believed him. Veronica gave him a brief smile, then turned away. She didn't want him to see the tears in her eyes. Tears brought on by the memory of her parents, by the violent death she'd witnessed so recently and by the hope that had her heart almost breaking.

GUNNER WATCHED AS the bodies were loaded into the back of the M.E.'s van. The M.E. had driven over from the county office as quickly as he could. Dr. Lawrence Tome had trembled when he touched the bodies with his gloved hands.

Gravel crunched behind him, but Gunner didn't

turn at the sound. He stared as the van pulled away, his eyes narrowed. The firefighters were still on-scene—volunteers—lingering as they surveyed the area. An arson investigator would be called in, but at the slow rate that things seemed to run in Whiskey Ridge, Gunner wasn't expecting any instant answers.

"You could have been killed." The low, angry and distinctly feminine voice was pitched to only reach his ears.

From the corner of his eye, he saw Sydney Sloan cross her arms over her chest, one of her angrier stances. Her short blond hair blew lightly in the breeze, tousling around her face. Her light green gaze wasn't on him. She was watching the firefighters. Or pretending to watch them.

He knew the full focus of her attention was on him. "The fire started and I had to—"

"I'm not talking about the fire. You ran *at* the shooter."

Ah, yes, she would have seen that. Especially since she'd been on surveillance duty.

"You didn't seek proper cover, Gunner. You didn't follow protocol, you didn't—"

"I'm not in the mood for a lecture." His words held a bite.

She sucked in a tight breath. "With me, you never seem to be in the mood for anything."

Now, what did she mean by that?

"You were gutted on the last case."

He winced at that, but yeah, it was the truth. He had the scars to prove it. So many scars.

"Now you're running headfirst at a killer? With no cover?" Her words held the snap of a whip. "Jasper was on the ground, covering the woman. He didn't have your back. You didn't wait for me or anyone else to come and help. You just…attacked."

Because he wasn't the kind to sit back and wait.

"If you've got some kind of death wish, you could be putting the whole team at risk."

The team. *His* team. The Shadow Agents who worked as a unit in the EOD. Sydney was part of his team. As was Jasper and their field leader, Logan Quinn. Jasper figured that Logan would be making an appearance soon, right after he finished his recon work in the area.

This case was big. Very, very big. All-hands-on-deck big. The EOD had sent in their best unit in order to find Cale Lane, and the Shadow Agents weren't going to stop until they brought the guy down.

*Shadow Agents.* They'd earned that nickname after their first few missions. No one had even seen them move in for their attack. *Move in like shadows. Make no sound. Attack. Leave without a trace.* That was the way the team worked. Normally.

This wasn't a normal situation. This time, they were hunting a killer who'd targeted some of their own. Other EOD agents. They weren't shadows this time. They were hunters who wanted their prey to be afraid.

"So do you have a death wish?" Sydney pressed, and she turned that deep gaze of hers on him. As always, when he stared in her eyes, he felt as if someone had just punched him in the gut.

Beautiful Sydney Sloan. Untouchable Sydney. Deadly Sydney.

"Worried about me?" He forced a mocking tone into his voice.

*"Yes."*

He wouldn't let his expression change. He'd always had to keep his guard up with her. *Off-limits.* Sydney wasn't for him. He knew that.

He didn't need his brother's ghost to remind him. But when he looked at her, he could almost hear Slade's voice. *"I know you want her, man. I've seen the way you look at her. But she's mine. She's going to marry me."*

Only Sydney hadn't married Gunner's brother. Because Slade Ortez had died in the jungle, and Gunner had been the man who pulled Sydney away from his body.

Gunner rolled his shoulders and forced his gaze from hers. The sheriff was pacing around the scene, looking furious. He was justified. Someone had just blown up his station. Gunner was surprised he was keeping any level of cool.

Sydney kept staring at him. Waiting. He could see her from the corner of his eye. The woman never gave up. Not on anything.

Or anyone.

"I don't have a death wish," Gunner told her quietly because it was obvious she wasn't going to let this drop. "So don't go running to Logan telling him I'm dangerous."

"That's *not* what I meant—"

He knew that. Sydney cared—*that* was the problem for them both. He tried to distract her, saying, "I didn't even realize you had surveillance set up last night." Now he felt as though he could glance back at her. "Tell me you caught sight of our killer." An image of Cale would cement the case against him.

She shook her head. "I'd just installed one camera. Thought it might be good to keep eyes on the station. I'd made it back to base and was testing the equipment when I saw—well, the flames were pretty hard to miss." Her voice dropped. "I saw the men fall, then I saw you take off. I knew I couldn't get to you fast enough."

"I can handle myself." She should know that.

"Can you?"

Before he could respond to what Gunner was sure had to be a deliberate taunt, the sheriff glanced his way. Then Wyatt began to march toward him.

"Wyatt Halliday," Sydney murmured. "Divorced, age thirty-four. Did a brief tour in the army, got a

BA in criminal justice from Texas A&M. Got shot in Dallas, almost died tracking a perp, and then the guy came out here. Guess he was looking for some peace and quiet."

Peace and quiet weren't on the day's agenda.

Wyatt huffed as he approached. "You." He jabbed a finger at Gunner. "We need to talk."

Gunner shrugged. Then he inclined his head toward Sydney. "This is Special Agent Sydney Sloan." That *was* her title at the EOD. He hadn't exactly lied to the sheriff just now. He was just letting him believe Sydney was a special agent with the FBI.

Wyatt hesitated. His gaze darted to Sydney. Lingered just a little too long for Gunner's comfort.

"You wanted to talk?" Gunner snapped, trying to draw Wyatt's attention away from Sydney.

Wyatt jerked his gaze back to Gunner. "I *want* to know what's going on. I got a friend at the bureau. I called him. He said there weren't any missing persons' cases that fit this attack profile, that he didn't know of a suspected perp who—"

Gunner raised his hand. "I'm not in town to investigate kidnappings. That was a cover I needed to give until we could get my team better established in Whiskey Ridge." Just like his cover with the FBI. But Sydney would have put safeguards in place for the FBI bit. If anyone investigated, if the sheriff got too curious, he'd find that there was a record for a

Special Agent Gunner Ortez and a record for Special Agent Sydney Sloan.

Sydney was always good at creating the covers.

"Then just why are you in town?" Wyatt pushed. "And why is my station destroyed?"

How much should he reveal? How much did the sheriff already know? It was hard to get a good read on the man.

"It's about Cale Lane, isn't it?" Wyatt dropped his voice and edged closer. "Veronica was right. Something has happened to him."

Not *to* him so much. With the sheriff's question, Gunner knew how to play the case now. "We are in town following up on Cale's disappearance."

Wyatt grunted. "I knew Veronica wouldn't give up. She called you in, didn't she?"

"Yes," Sydney said. "She got our attention."

Well, Gunner knew that the lady had certainly gotten Jasper's attention.

Wyatt glanced over his shoulder at the charred remains of his station. "What Cale does, it's dangerous. He knows the risks that he takes, but I don't think Veronica ever really understood just how deadly his job could be."

Gunner frowned as he got what Wyatt was saying and what he wasn't saying. "He asked you to cover for him." A hunch.

Wyatt gave a grim nod and cut his eyes back to Gunner. "Said he'd be gone longer this time. That the money—it was enough for him to get out of the business."

The sheriff hadn't cared that Cale was a hired gun?

"Don't look that way," Wyatt said, voice fierce. "He was working for Uncle Sam. Same as you. Same as me...back before the shooting."

Wyatt had done mercenary work, too?

"Cale said he'd be gone longer, that the case was big. I thought he was just still working the job. I didn't realize—" He broke off and shook his head. "Cale Lane is my best friend. Do you really think I'd turn my back on him if I thought he was in trouble?"

It didn't matter what he thought. It only mattered what the evidence showed. All of their evidence was currently showing that Cale was the killer who'd taken out three EOD agents—and that he was quite possibly the man who'd shot the two suspects last night.

"I want you to tell me everything you know about Cale Lane," Gunner said. "Every. Single. Thing."

Because if they were going to catch Cale before the man killed again, then they had to get inside his mind.

To catch a killer, you had to think like one.

## Chapter Four

"Why isn't anyone else here?"

Veronica jumped and spun around, her heart racing. Jasper stood in the kitchen doorway, wearing a pair of faded jeans that clung low on his waist.

And nothing else.

His chest rippled with muscles. His shoulders filled that doorway, and Veronica had to yank her jaw off the floor.

"Veronica? Why's the ranch deserted?"

"B-because it's not a working ranch." Not yet. But Cale had talked about changing that. "Cale and I—we bought it for the privacy." *The isolation.* "We have a few horses, and someone comes in to tend to them, but…"

But it was just her.

Alone with Jasper.

"Where do you work?" he asked as his gaze swept over her.

Like him, she was dressed in old jeans, but she also had on a T-shirt. He needed a shirt. Her gaze kept falling to his chest. "My office is down the hallway. Third door."

"You do all your work from the ranch?"

She nodded. "I've got a satellite connection for the internet—that connection is all I need." She built websites for doctors, lawyers, schools, writers. Anyone who needed the sites designed and maintained.

And she did it without having to rush to the city or having to face off with clients.

She had a partner in Dallas who took care of the PR and marketing end of things. Kelly booked the clients, found out just what they needed, and Veronica did the building and website coding part of the business.

It was a deal that worked well for them both.

"You shouldn't be out here alone." Now Jasper sounded angry.

"I've got a security system." One that she would *not* be forgetting to activate ever again. "I'm perfectly safe."

"Out here by yourself? In the middle of nowhere? If you needed help, who would get to you before you were dead?"

Now, that was a brutal jab she hadn't seen coming.

He stalked toward her. "Who would get to you," he demanded, voice lowering, "if you needed help right now?"

Her hands were behind her. Curling around the

counter. "I'm not as defenseless as you seem to think." He was trying to scare her. She got that.

"Aren't you?" Jasper pressed.

She grabbed the knife that she'd just used and yanked it in front of her. "No, I'm not."

He smiled, and she had the impression that she'd actually surprised him.

She doubted that much surprised Jasper.

But then the crazy man grabbed the knife. No, he grabbed her hand as it held the knife's handle. "Having a weapon and being willing to use it are two different things." His breath blew lightly over her. "Would you be willing to kill?"

No. "I'm not looking to kill anyone."

"What if someone wants to kill you?" He lifted her hand to the counter. She dropped the knife. "Gunner called me," Jasper told her. "He can't reveal everything about the case, but those two men who were shot last night? They were hired thugs. Their prints came back and matched to a Billy Ferrell and Chuck Trout. They've got a dozen charges on them in Dallas. B and E, assault…"

"Kidnapping?"

"No. Looks like you're their first kidnap attempt. But word is that those guys weren't afraid to hire out their services."

"You're saying…" She licked her lips. His gaze dropped, heated. He felt the awareness, too. That was a good thing, right? "You're saying they were hired to take me?"

"Gunner found out that Trout's older brother served in a training unit with Cale. Back when the men first enlisted. The guy died in combat, but Cale just might have kept in touch with his family."

"How does Gunner know this already?" It was just past nine in the morning.

"Because the team is good."

The team? The FBI?

"The team might be good," she managed. "But you're wrong about Cale. He wouldn't pay someone to kidnap me. That doesn't even make sense."

"You're asking a lot of questions about his whereabouts. Turning over rocks that might need to stay still. Maybe he got tired of that scrutiny."

"*No.* This is my brother—I know what I'm talking about. He didn't hire those men." They'd had knives. They'd forced her car off the road. No way would Cale have sent them after her.

Jasper held her gaze a beat longer. "*Someone* hired them."

"Let Gunner and Wyatt find that someone." She couldn't lose her focus. "We have to find Cale." She waited a beat and then, because he'd pushed her buttons and tried to make her doubt the one person who had always been there for her, Veronica said, "That is what I'm paying you for."

One blond brow climbed. "So it is."

He backed up. She could breathe again.

"And here I thought you might be interested in other…things."

He was talking about the kiss. Her cheeks flushed. Seriously. He'd just brought that up? To her face? "I was stressed."

"Um."

"Adrenaline was surging. I—I didn't even know what I was doing."

"Sure seemed like you knew to me." His gaze dipped to her mouth. "If you feel the urge to…have another surge, you let me know."

She couldn't even think of a comeback.

"Until then, I've got some leads to run down."

Leads? "I'm coming with you."

His gaze narrowed. "After last night, there's no way I'd leave you behind. Someone's targeting you—and until Gunner catches that someone, you're gonna have yourself a full-time guard."

"Th-that's not what I'm paying you for." What if he wanted more money? Her resources were close to being tapped out.

But he flashed her a wide smile, one that made her heart feel a little funny. "Consider it a bonus," he said.

*"He's a tough SOB."* She remembered the words Cale had spoken to her the one time she'd met the two men at a restaurant in Dallas. He'd given her the warning when Jasper had slipped away to take

a phone call. Her gaze must have lingered on Jasper's back for a little too long because her brother had leaned in to tell her... *"Don't make the mistake of thinking there's anything soft in there. A guy like him would eat you up and spit you out."*

Jasper's gaze was a little too knowing on her.

*Eat you up.*

She gulped. "L-let's go." She tried to head for the door.

He grabbed her arm. "Aren't you going to ask about them?"

*Them?* She knew what he meant, of course. Her gaze lowered to his chest. To the dozens of scars that crisscrossed his tanned flesh. "You survived." Simple. The marks didn't detract from his appeal. They just made him look tougher, stronger. The scars were silent testament to all that he'd survived. "Is there more you want to tell me?"

Because she would listen.

He shook his head. "I don't get you. Earlier, I thought I was— *I don't get you.*"

Most people didn't. Story of her life. But she tried to keep her voice light as she said, "What's to get?" She wanted to lift her hand and trace the white ridge of the scar on his shoulder. Or let her fingers slide over the still-red scar on his stomach. A long, thick red line that looked dangerously fresh. "You're a survivor."

"Most women get... They don't like the scars."

She forced herself to hold his stare. "I'm not m-most women." Nothing about him was a turnoff to her. No, he turned her on too much. More than any other man ever had. He was lethal in so many ways.

"No" was his quiet, thoughtful reply. "You aren't."

Her hands had fisted. The better not to touch him. But now she saw the curiosity in his eyes. The kind of curiosity a man got when he found a woman he wanted.

Her breath caught. She didn't know what to do right now. Stand there, kiss him or run.

Since she was largely a coward at heart, she ran. Or at least, she walked very, very quickly from the room.

And felt his gaze follow her every step.

VERONICA STUTTERED WHEN she was nervous. He seemed to make her nervous a whole lot.

Jasper kinda liked her stutter. It was a little sweet and oddly sexy.

But he didn't have time to think about her sexy stutter then. For the moment, he had to keep his thoughts on the case.

Despite the news that Gunner had given him about the would-be kidnappers, Jasper wasn't going to head out of town with Veronica. Sure, it looked as though the trail might be leading to Dallas, but the shooter had been in Whiskey Ridge hours before. He'd been right there. So Jasper was betting that he was still around. The shooter had just gone to ground.

Gotten cover.

For the time being.

"Why are we going back to Last Chance?" Veronica asked him, and he saw her tense as she glanced out of the window and toward the smashed fence.

Had last night's wreck reminded her of the hell she'd faced as a child? He wanted to ask her, but Jasper knew he'd pushed her too much already.

"Your brother had a contact at Last Chance." This much was true. Jasper also wanted to make sure that *contact* saw him with Veronica. All the better to bait his trap.

"How do you know that?"

*Lie, lie, lie.* "Because I recognized him when I went into the bar last night."

"Another army buddy?"

"Something like that." More like a guy who'd gone AWOL and gotten tossed in the brig. A guy who knew how to deal dirty.

Jasper had been surprised to spot the man there, and if Veronica hadn't been in danger, he would have pushed the guy for information before he'd left last night.

"It's the middle of the day. No one is even gonna be in Last Chance now." Veronica's lack of hope was obvious.

But he knew something she didn't. "The owner will be there."

She turned her head. Frowned.

"He's the one we want." They were past the accident scene now. Good. It looked as though she was even breathing better.

Jasper glanced in the rearview mirror. No tails. Nothing but empty road.

"Why...why were you fighting last night?"

Ah, he'd almost forgotten about that little incident. "The guy thought he could get rough with a waitress." His hands tightened around the steering wheel. "He thought wrong."

"So you decided to beat the right thought into him?" She sounded censuring.

What response had he expected from her? "No, I told the guy to back the hell off, but when he took a swing at me, I swung back." He glanced toward her. Found that bright stare on him. "I always swing back."

"I know."

He frowned at that.

"Cale told me a few things about you."

He had? Jasper eased up on the accelerator. He wanted to hear this. "What did he say?"

"Mostly that I should stay away from you."

So Cale *had* seen the way he looked at Veronica. One meeting. One two-hour dinner in Dallas on a night that felt like a lifetime ago. She'd been wearing a blue dress that made her eyes even brighter. Her hair had been pulled back. She'd smelled like honeysuckles then, too. He'd looked at her...

*And wanted.*

When she'd excused herself for a moment, Cale had leaned close. *"She's not for you."* That had been all he had said to him.

But it seemed he might have said plenty more to her.

"Why'd he tell you to stay away?" Because he was curious and annoyed. The chemistry between him and Veronica was so hot it almost burned him every time she got near. For her brother to keep shoving her in the opposite direction...

"He said you were too much like him. Too dark. Too wary of commitment. You weren't the kind of guy who'd go for the picket-fence routine."

Because he didn't know what the picket-fence routine was. He'd sure never grown up in that perfect world of baseball games and barbecues. He didn't know a damn thing about that life. So how could he ever give it to a woman like Veronica?

"You always do what Cale tells you to do?"

She didn't speak for a moment; then she said, "I'm here with you now, aren't I?"

Yes, she was. He wouldn't let his lips curl in satisfaction. *She's a job. Don't forget that.* But he could feel himself starting to slide down the slippery slope that would lead to lust and sex and pleasure.

*Want her.*

He also had one more question for her. "Just how did you know that I was going to be at Last Chance?" Another long curve, and then he could see the bar and its empty parking lot, standing stark on the barren landscape.

"It's a small town." She shrugged. The seat belt slid over her shoulder. "Word travels fast."

*That fast?*

She slanted him a look from the corner of her eye. "I actually saw you in Tom's Diner, but you left before I could approach you. Since there is only one motel in town, it didn't take me long to track you down."

He waited.

"Once I, uh, 'confirmed' with the clerk where you were staying, it wasn't hard to figure out that you'd headed to the only bar in the county."

Then she'd put on her sexy clothes—damn sexy—and come calling for him. Made him an offer that he couldn't refuse.

Interesting. The woman was resourceful. He'd remember that.

He pulled into the lot. Checked his rearview mirror once more. No one for miles.

"You're sure the bartender's here?" Veronica asked as she pressed her fingertips against the dashboard.

"I scoped the place last night." He could be plenty

resourceful, too. "There's an apartment out back. We'll find Reed there." Reed Montgomery. Bartender. Bar owner. Broker of mercenaries. The guy was a jack-of-all-trades. He was also wanted in about four countries. No wonder the guy had set up shop in a place called Last Chance. Of course, he was using an alias. That alias was why Jasper and his team hadn't realized that the guy was even in this game, not until Jasper had laid eyes on the fellow last night. Reed's real name was Thomas Jensen. Jensen was still wanted by the U.S. government... that little matter of being AWOL wasn't just going to vanish.

Veronica shoved open her door. He waited a moment, grabbed the backup gun he'd retrieved from his bag and tucked it under the waistband of his jeans. He pulled his shirt down to cover the gun, but if anyone looked close enough, that person would see the bulge of his weapon.

He shut the door, making sure not to slam it. Reed was a facilitator in the business. The kind of guy with too many contacts. One who loved providing work to down-on-their-luck cowboys and soldiers. Dangerous work.

Cigarette butts littered the ground. Through the small windows, he saw that the bar's interior was dim and silent. He passed the bar, not slowing. Veronica's quiet footsteps followed him.

"Are you sure he's our guy?" she whispered.

Jasper grunted. "You hired me for my contacts, didn't you?" Only she didn't know that the contacts in question had actually come from the EOD. Sydney had done the intel on this one. Once Jasper had ID'd Reed, Sydney had linked the guy to Cale. For the past five years, Cale had always visited the bar just days before he went out on a mission. He *never* came into the bar any other time.

Just right before he deployed. Five days before each mission, to be precise. Like clockwork.

Sydney had riffled through Cale's credit-card records in order to find that little nugget of information.

At the apartment door, Jasper hesitated. He didn't want to leave Veronica out in the open, but he also didn't want her to see just how hard he might have to push Reed.

*I can't take him down in front of her. It will blow my cover.*

But he also wasn't about to let the guy get away. Not if this little Q and A went down the way he thought it would.

His gaze flickered to her. She stared at him, then mouthed, *I'm coming with you.*

Well, situation settled. Nodding grimly, he lifted his hand and slammed his fist into the door. "Reed Montgomery, open the door. My name's Jasper Adams. I need to—"

The door swung inward. Because it wasn't locked.

Because it wasn't even shut all the way and the force of Jasper's fist had sent the wood sliding in.

The interior of the apartment seemed as dim and silent as the bar.

"Reed?" he called out, raising his voice.

No response.

But he'd seen Reed's motorcycle parked outside the apartment. Sydney had tagged the vehicle so that Jasper would know what ride to look for at the scene.

He took a step inside.

Veronica grabbed his arm. "You can't just walk in there," she said, voice hushed. "That's against the law! That's breaking and entering."

He exhaled slowly. "It's not breaking if the door is wide open."

She blinked.

"Besides, this *is* why you hired me." No way was he about to let this perfect opportunity slip by him. He took her wrist and pulled her inside behind him. She shut the door, looking pale but determined.

Her first B and E, well, E. Cute.

He glanced around. All of the blinds were down, so they didn't have to worry about anyone taking a shot at them right then. The shooter would never be able to get a clear hit without seeing into the apartment. Jasper began to advance, surveying the area. Everything seemed to be in place. No furniture overturned. TV turned off. Breakfast...

Still out.

Jasper froze. A half-eaten pancake with congealed syrup waited on the kitchen table. "Reed?" he called one more time even as his nose twitched. The smell in the place was off. The deeper he went into the apartment, the thicker that slightly rancid odor became.

He paused in front of a closed door. Had to be for the bedroom because the bathroom was right next to the little den. Before he turned the knob, Jasper took out his gun and cradled it carefully in his right hand. No sounds came from inside that room. Not even a whisper of sound.

He opened the door.

*Because the dead can't whisper.*

Reed Montgomery was most definitely dead.

The man's body was lying facedown on the floor. Blood had pooled beneath him. His hands were out by his sides, positioned deliberately.

Jasper knew that if he turned the man over, he'd find that the guy's throat had been sliced. The killer had come up on the guy, walked silently up behind him, caught him off guard…

And used his knife on Reed's throat. The man wouldn't have even had the chance to scream. Not that a scream would have helped him.

*Just like the others.* Because Jasper had looked at a crime scene like this before. Three times before.

"Jasper." Veronica's strangled voice. He glanced

at her, saw the horror on her face. The increased pallor of her skin.

Hell. Another dead body for her to deal with in less than twenty-four hours.

He blocked her view. "Go back into the den." He needed to search the scene. He couldn't risk her contaminating evidence, and he just...

*I don't want her having to stare at the body.*

"It's him, isn't it?" She swallowed. "The man who owns the bar. The one you called Reed."

He nodded.

"I...talked to him last night. He's the one who directed me to you when I came in Last Chance."

So Reed had recognized him, too. Jasper had suspected that the man remembered him. Reed would also have known that Veronica was Cale's sister. No way would the guy not be aware of her, not after all of his dealings with Cale. So Reed had realized that Jasper and Veronica were hooking up; he'd probably figured that Jasper was helping to track Cale.

Just hours after he'd gotten that knowledge, he had been killed.

Killed...*silenced.*

*The killer knew I was coming to talk to Reed.*

So Reed had been taken out.

"He asked me...asked if I was sure I wanted you." Her gaze was on his. "I was sure." Her chin lifted. "Is he dead...because of whatever is happening with Cale?"

Why lie? Besides, the woman already knew the truth. "Looks that way."

He gave her credit. She didn't flinch. Her shoulders straightened, and she turned for the door. She'd taken two steps when she hesitated. "Did he suffer?"

"No." The kill had been quick and clean. The work of a man who knew just what he was doing with a knife.

"Good." Her breath whispered out. "My father... he suffered... No one should have to suffer." She slipped from the room.

Swearing, Jasper turned back to the body. He yanked out his phone. Punched one button to get Gunner on the line. "I'm going to need a crime-scene team out at Last Chance," he said, not bothering to identify himself. "Our guy's struck again."

A swift inhalation of air, and then Gunner demanded, "You're sure it's the one we're looking for?"

"No sign of B and E." Not from what he could tell. *Just like the other scenes.* "Looks like the victim let him in." The kill had happened just hours before. "Then when the vic turned his back, the killer struck." His fingers tightened on the phone. "The attack came from behind, just like the others. A slice right across the jugular. The victim bled out." Had it been easy? Had he suffered?

He sure would never tell Veronica if the guy had. The last thing she needed to know was just how sadistic Cale could be.

"Get our medical examiner in on this." They'd fly Dr. Sarah Jacobs in. No local with shaking hands would handle this kill. "I'm betting that once the crime-scene guys go over this, and she gets to see the body, all the results will be the same as before."

The results...the info that the techs gathered about the killer's height and weight and military training... all based on the kill method.

Height...approximately six foot three. Tall enough that he had to slice downward when his hand curled around the victims' necks.

Weight...two hundred pounds. He'd left shoe imprints in clay outside one of the vic's homes. *The killer's mistakes.* Uncle Sam's crime-scene team could do some damn incredible things with their technology. Like...

Determine the guy's weight based on the depth of those impressions. Get the man's height based on the length between his steps and the size of the shoe. A height that had matched dead-on with the M.E.'s estimates.

The killer had even left one other valuable piece of info behind in those shoe impressions. A few bits of clay that could be tracked back to only a handful of locations in the U.S....and one of those locations was right here in Whiskey Ridge.

The killer had screwed up on that second kill. When he'd gone after Julian Forrest, an ex-marine, the killer had counted on the forecasted prediction of rain to wipe away his footprints.

That rain hadn't come.

*Did you screw up this time, too?*

He was about to find out.

Jasper exhaled. "The kill's fresh," he told Gunner. "We need our team searching the area. Cale Lane *is* here, and unless I'm wrong, it sure looks like he's trying to cover his tracks."

By killing.

Because Reed Montgomery wasn't like the last three victims that had been killed in their homes. Victims who'd opened the door to the killer because they had known him.

*They all knew Cale.* In one way or another, those three victims had all traced back to Cale. One of the men had trained with him in Georgia. Another had been on a mission with Cale in Syria. One had worked with Cale for a month in an African desert.

All three of those victims had been EOD. They'd been executed.

Reed…he'd been executed, too, but not because he was EOD. He'd died for another reason. *To protect the killer's identity.*

Jasper ended the call. *He killed you because of what you knew.*

Now Jasper just needed to find the evidence that Reed had possessed. Evidence that had been worth killing for.

CALE LANE WATCHED the house, his eyes narrowed as his fingers curled around his weapon. He preferred to use a knife on his kills. Much quieter than a gun. More personal. You were able to get right up to your target. With a knife, there would be no mistakes. No miscalculations on those up-close kills.

Jasper Adams knew all about close kills. The man had been killing for over ten years.

And now that man was with his sister. Cale had seen them go into the apartment together. Seen the way Jasper's fingers lingered on Veronica's arm.

He'd warned Jasper to stay away from her.

Jasper should have listened to him.

Now his old buddy was going to get caught in the bloody battle. There was nothing Cale could do to change fate. Death was coming. No, death had already taken over Whiskey Ridge. He could feel its dark shadow all around him.

The only thing to do now… Cale had to make sure the blood that spilled didn't belong to his sister. But anyone else…

*Fair game.*

# Chapter Five

The computer was just sitting there. Okay, not so much sitting as hiding beneath a pile of papers. But as Veronica paced the small den, she caught sight of the laptop, and before she could think of the million reasons why she shouldn't open it, she was on the couch, the laptop in her hands.

Immediately, the password screen popped up. Her eyes narrowed. She didn't know Reed. Knew nothing about him except...

*Last Chance.* She typed the letters quickly, not looking at the keys. Her gaze darted back to the hallway. Jasper was still in there, with the body.

Her stomach churned. There had been so much blood.

*Don't think about him. Don't. Build that wall of ice again. Don't feel. Don't. Feel.*

Three dead bodies. At least she hadn't seen the light go out of Reed's eyes.

But she'd looked at him, at his long body, and for an instant, she'd seen her brother.

*Cale isn't dead.*

And Last Chance wasn't the right password.

Of course, would it ever be that easy?

Her gaze flew around the room. Looking for something, anything to help her. Most people used passwords that reminded them of things they loved. Kids' names, hobbies, favorite books, favorite—

There was a big poster of John Wayne on the guy's wall.

The Duke was the password that let her in to his system.

Her shoulders hunched as she curled over the screen. Her fingers typed, faster and faster as she searched through the material. Files had been deleted, recently, too, but the person deleting hadn't known what he was doing. Sure, he'd sent the material to the trash, then deleted the trash, but...

*That wasn't good enough.*

Two more clicks of her fingers and she had the "deleted" files open.

One file was titled "Chances." She clicked it and frowned as she read. It looked like a series of jobs. Not so much jobs as...maybe missions. Locations were listed. Dates. Then some sort of code names. Razor. Jumper. Deuce. Striker Two.

"What are you doing?"

She jumped. Jasper had come back. Moved so silently that she'd never even heard him enter the room. Cale was the only other man she knew who could move like that.

Her heart was in her throat, but she swallowed and managed to shove it back down where it belonged. "I found Reed's laptop and recovered some files." She frowned up at him. "He doesn't name the men who've been working his jobs. They all have code names."

His lips tightened. "There could be prints on that laptop."

Prints. She hadn't even—

"Put it down, carefully. Crime-scene techs will be coming soon."

They'd find her prints all over the machine. Wonderful. Prints at a crime scene. Witness to two murders hours before. This wasn't exactly the exciting life that she'd always craved.

Gingerly, she put the laptop on the old coffee table. "He lists names like Deuce, Razor, Striker—"

"Striker is the code name that your brother used."

And her heart was right back in her throat. Her gaze flew to the screen. "His last job was... It was just three weeks ago. In...Phoenix?" That didn't make any sense. "What kind of job would he be doing there?"

"You really don't know him that well," Jasper murmured.

Goose bumps rose on her arms. She stood, shaking. "Do you know what kind of job took him there?" She rubbed her forehead. "He saved people. That's what he told me. He took rescue missions. When tourists were kidnapped and held for ransom, their parents couldn't always pay, so *he* went in." She didn't like what Jasper was implying. "Cale is a hero," she said again.

Jasper didn't speak then. In that stark silence, Veronica wasn't sure…was she trying to convince him that her brother was a good man or was she trying to convince herself?

"I've seen names like these before," she whispered. Not those exact names, but similar ones. She rubbed a hand over her forehead. "They were scribbled on the backs of some old photos that Cale had at the house and—" She broke off, her eyes widening. *"I'd seen him before."*

Jasper frowned at her.

"The tattoo on Reed's arm." She barely breathed the words. "That's why it caught my eye at Last Chance. I—I'd seen it…in one of the pictures at the ranch." She thought about Reed's face, took ten years away from it, gave him hair… "He served with my brother."

"That's how they connected. How Reed knew that Cale could get the jobs done for him."

Jasper had recognized Reed, too. He'd remembered the man from the military, and Jasper had known just what sort of business Cale had been involved with at the bar.

Before she could figure out what to say next, she heard the growl of a car's engine. Jasper tensed, and his hand went to his waist—and to the gun tucked in his waistband.

Then he was moving silently toward the door. Pushing aside the shade and peering outside. After a brief moment, the tension left his shoulders. "It's the good guys."

For some reason, it was getting harder for her to tell the difference between the good guys and the bad guys.

Jasper glanced back at her. "Gunner's team is in town. When I found the body, I called them." He paused a beat, then said, "You can trust them."

She shook her head. "*You're* the only one I trust."

He gazed back at her. A faint furrow appeared between his brows.

"Why didn't you just call the sheriff?" she asked. "Wyatt would—"

"This case is a little over his head. And the station blew up last night. He's already got enough to deal with." He tucked the gun back in his waistband. "If the agents need his help, they'll say so."

She pushed her hands against the tops of her thighs. She was sweating, far too nervous and far too aware of the dead body down the hallway.

Then the front door opened. A tall, dark man with short black hair and a faint scar under his chin marched inside. He seemed to fill the small room, dominating the space. Between him and Jasper, she suddenly felt very, very overwhelmed.

Then the stranger's gaze turned toward her. "You're Veronica Lane."

She nodded.

"I'm Agent Logan Quinn." He offered his hand.

She took it slowly and immediately had her fingers clasped in a warm, strong grip.

Then she was free. Logan glanced at Jasper. "Glad you were on this one, man. If she'd wandered in alone…"

Her spine straightened. "I would have managed to call the authorities just fine on my own."

Logan's eyelids flickered. "Of course, my apologies, you would have, but if the body's as fresh as Jasper says, then the killer may still be close by."

Just what she didn't need to hear.

"Let's ease out of here until the techs arrive." Logan waved toward the door.

Unable to help herself, Veronica cast a longing look toward the laptop.

"Don't worry, we'll take care of that," Logan told her.

Yes, that was what she was afraid of.

Veronica nodded even as she curled her hand over the small flash drive that had been attached to the laptop. The flash drive that she'd taken the liberty of "borrowing"—right after she'd copied those recovered files. The files had been saved to the flash drive just seconds before Jasper had appeared in the den.

The sunlight hit her the minute she stepped outside the apartment. Spring, but it was still already uncomfortably warm. Veronica was surprised to see a few other cars there. Her gaze scanned the lot. She recognized Gunner. Beside him stood a woman with short blond hair and fierce eyes. A few people in suits were scattered around the area.

"We'll let the crime techs take over while we do a little…hunting in the area."

Logan's voice was mild, but his use of the word *hunting* seemed strange to her. She looked over at him, frowning.

"You need some help with that?" Jasper asked, his own voice just as mild.

Logan hesitated, then glanced her way. "We got this covered. Why don't you just finish your business with Ms. Lane."

She didn't think that she liked Logan Quinn. His gaze was too guarded. His words were too careful. She had the impression that he was a man who carried secrets, a *lot* of them.

Veronica took a few steps toward Jasper's truck; then she hesitated. Her instincts were screaming at her. She looked over her shoulder at the agent. "Logan, do you know my brother?" She wasn't going to "Mr. Quinn" him.

She caught the flicker of surprise on his face. "Yes, I do."

Her heart iced. Suddenly, everything was making a whole lot of sense to her.

The agents' presence in town. At least two agents from the FBI...both in little Whiskey Ridge. All of those guys in suits. The fast response to Jasper's call.

When they'd been at the police station, Gunner had insisted on questioning her kidnappers—questioning them alone.

*He hadn't wanted to say anything in front of me.*

And now Cale's code name had been the last one listed in Reed's deleted files.

She had to face the facts, even if those facts scared her to death. It wasn't just a coincidence that the federal agents were in town. The agents were in Whiskey Ridge because they were hunting Cale.

She reached for Jasper's hand, pulled him close. "W-we'll stay out of your way. Don't worry." Because she and Jasper were going to hunt and *find* Cale long before the agents could.

Jasper stiffened a bit at her touch, but she just curled her arm around him more. Then she started pulling him away from that apartment that smelled of death and away from the agent with suspicious eyes.

They didn't speak until they were inside Jasper's truck. He turned on the engine, and his gaze flickered toward Gunner and Logan.

The agents who were staring right back at them.

"I know what you said," she began quietly as her hands clenched in her lap. "But I *can't* trust them."

His gaze darted to her.

"Don't you see what's happening?" she demanded. "They think that my brother is a killer. They're tracking him down because they want to *take* him down."

"Veronica…"

"Are you working with them?" The question had to be asked. Gunner and Logan both knew Jasper. Jasper knew Cale. It would be foolish of her to ignore the coincidence. But…

*I trust him.*

Her heart seemed to stop as she waited for Jasper's response.

"I'm working for *you*." Anger roughened the words. "Until last night, I was taking a break, enjoying a little R and R in a spot on the map that I thought most folks didn't even know about."

A spot Cale must have told him about.

Jasper's stare seemed to burn into her. "I'm not FBI."

She could see the truth in his gaze.

"I swear, I'm not part of the bureau."

Why would he lie?

"I am going to help you find Cale. The agents… I'm going to use every connection that I have to them and—"

"They're hunting my brother." Would he deny that?

A muscle jerked along his jaw. "They're hunting a killer."

Did he think Cale was that killer? Did it even matter to him?

She licked her lips. "You might know them, you might have worked with them before, but don't trust them, either, okay?"

He put the truck into Drive and pulled away from the apartment. They passed two unmarked vans. Her body tensed at that sight. The agents were pulling in all kinds of resources on this case.

*My brother didn't kill Reed.*

She had to find her brother before the agents did. Logan Quinn scared her, and she didn't want that man hunting her brother.

Cale wasn't the killer. She'd prove that fact *and* find her brother.

"YOUR BROTHER'S IN town." Jasper made this announcement as soon as they pulled through the gates at her ranch after a silent ride back.

He parked the truck on the side of the graveled drive and turned to face her. The better to catch her reaction.

*She thinks Logan and Gunner are after her brother. But she doesn't suspect me. Why?*

*Why the hell does she trust me so much?*

Part of him was humbled by that trust. No one

had ever had such blind faith in him before. But another part, a darker part, was angry.

He was going to betray that trust. Break it. Break her.

*That's not what I want.*

She jerked free of the seat belt. "Don't you start this. Don't tell me that Cale is a killer!"

That hadn't been what he intended to say, but yes, all signs sure pointed to the fact that Cale was very much a killer.

Veronica pushed open the door and hopped out of the truck.

Where was she going?

He killed the engine and followed her. "Veronica!"

It looked as if she was planning on leaving his butt and walking the rest of the way back to the ranch.

At his call, she didn't stop walking. He ran to her, caught her arm and forced her around to face him. He was leaning over her, their faces close. Her cheeks were angry, flushed.

Damn if he didn't want to kiss her.

She'd kissed him before. Didn't that mean it was his turn? Turn or not…

He took her mouth.

She didn't fight, didn't gasp, didn't try to pull away.

Veronica stood on her toes, shocking the hell out

of him, and she kissed him back. Kissed him back with passion and fury and lust.

Enough lust to make a man ache.

His hands eased down her body, curled around the flare of her hips, and he lifted her up against his aroused flesh. She turned him on more than any other woman ever had. *With just a kiss.* He wanted her.

Naked.

Eager.

And whispering his name as pleasure flashed in her eyes.

Her tongue slid over his lip in a move so sweet and sexy that she had him growling. The woman was getting beneath his skin. Making him want, when he should be focusing on the job.

He *never* lost focus. He got the job done, no matter what. He *always* finished the mission.

He licked her lip. Thrust his tongue into her mouth.

Her taste drove him insane, made him crave more of her. So much more. His blood seemed to burn in his veins as arousal hardened his body.

Time to get a few things straight. He lifted his mouth from hers, but didn't let her go. He was enjoying having his hands on her far too much for that. "I'm not taking your money."

She blinked. There was desire in her eyes. The

desire deepened the blue color. Made her even sexier. "But we had a deal."

The deal was getting real complicated, fast. The deal was also based on a lie.

Lying to her was becoming harder each moment.

"Things have changed." He wasn't the coldhearted bastard so many people seemed to think.

Since when did it matter what anyone thought?

Not anyone. *Her.* "People are dying in this town, left and right."

Her arms were on his shoulders. When he'd kissed her, Veronica's nails had bit into his skin.

He'd liked that. When they had sex, and they *were* going to get naked together, he wanted her wild.

*Business. Focus on business.*

But now her hands were trying to ease away from him. She was easing away. "Are you scared?" She seemed shocked by the idea. "I mean, I understand, I'm scared, too. I don't want to die—"

"Not happening." The words ripped from him automatically. Hell, no, she wasn't dying. Not on his watch.

Her gaze held his. "It's okay if you want to leave." Her hands dropped. "You have to look after yourself. When w-we made the deal, you didn't know you were signing on to something that would involve three murders and a kidnapping in less than twenty-four hours—"

He kissed her. He didn't want her backing away

from him, and he sure didn't want her trying to build a wall between them. So Jasper poured his hunger and need into the kiss. Let her know that this wasn't some hired gun's deal. This was a man, wanting a woman. Wanting *her*.

His right hand rose from the curve of her hip. Rose to cup her jaw. When his mouth finally pulled from hers—she'd been as eager to keep that kiss going as he had been—Jasper tilted her chin up to make sure she kept her focus on him.

*And not on trying to flee.*

"The deal isn't gonna work," he told her, "because right now my priority isn't on finding your brother."

"But—"

"It's on keeping you safe."

A faint line appeared between her eyes.

"I'll be doing that job, no pay, got it? I'll keep looking for your brother because I'm not leaving you on your own. It's too dangerous. You need help, and I'm right here to help you." And to do anything else to her that she'd let him do.

His fingers caressed her skin. Then he let her go.

With a shake of her head, Veronica said, "Why would a guy like you protect me for free?"

He stiffened at that. "A guy like me?" Weren't they past this by now?

"I—I'm sorry, I didn't—"

His jaw locking, he gritted, "I'm more than just the soldier you met years ago."

"I know that." Soft, then, as if confessing, "I've seen that truth in your eyes."

He wondered just what else he might have revealed to her. Curious, he asked her, "What do you see in my eyes now?"

She licked her lips. "You want me." Veronica seemed surprised by that. Why?

The woman was sexy as hell. Even wearing jeans instead of that come-get-me short skirt she'd worn at the bar—a skirt that had sure fueled some fantasies for him.

As for wanting her...

"Damn straight," Jasper told her, his voice deepening. He could have been more blunt. But he held back what he wanted to do with her. The woman looked nervous enough as it was.

"So you...aren't going to accept my money?"

He nodded.

"But you aren't leaving."

Another nod.

The furrow was still between her brows as she asked, "Y-you're going to be some kind of—of what? Bodyguard?"

"If that's how you want to think of me."

She looked so lost and confused that he wanted to kiss her again.

"Why?" Veronica gave a little shake of her head. "Because you think that by playing hero, you'll get me into bed?"

*Playing hero?* He hadn't realized he was playing at anything. "No, ma'am," he finally drawled, "that wasn't what I was thinking." He raised a brow. "If I get you in bed with me, it's because you want to be there, no other reason."

Her breath rushed out.

"As for finding your brother, I'll still help you do that, but I never should have agreed to take your money." And here was another confession, one that was eating at him. "Especially since I owe Cale." Owing Cale made the whole mess even more tangled.

"Why do you owe him?"

"He saved my life." It was hard to repay a debt like that. Especially when you were the guy in charge of bringing down the man who'd hauled your butt out of a South American jungle as bullets flew around you. "One of our early missions…didn't go so well." Because he'd been taken in by an innocent face. A woman who'd begged for help.

He'd wanted to help her.

Too late, he'd realized she was the bait to draw in his team so that the rebels in the area could attack. The first bullet had almost taken his heart. It *had* taken him out, because he'd fallen to the ground as blood pumped from him.

Cale had grabbed him. Fired his gun again and again. Gotten them both to safety.

*As payment, here I am, hunting you, and planning to take your sister to bed.*

Cale backed away from her. "I'm sorry."

She blinked.

He did have some shred of conscience left. He'd thought he'd lost that years ago, but here it was, rearing its head. Maybe he could even do the right thing. Maybe. Jasper forced himself to say, "I shouldn't have kissed you, shouldn't have touched you." His voice sounded wooden now because the memory of blood and thick vegetation and a friend's strong arm around his shoulders was too vivid in his mind. He did owe Cale, and even though he was going to bring the other man in, he couldn't betray him this way, too.

*No matter how much I want her.* Images of Veronica had been haunting him. He wanted her so much his whole body ached, and the thought of having her naked…

*Yes.*

But he could still hear the sound of those bullets flying in the jungle.

*Stay in control.* Wasn't he already betraying her enough? The white-hot lust he felt, that stark awareness between them, could just wind up hurting them both. Cale didn't want to hurt Veronica.

Cale motioned toward the truck. "Get in. We'll head back to the house. Figure out our next move."

It took him a few moments to realize that she wasn't moving. He glanced back at her. "Veronica?"

Her hands went to her hips. "I didn't know you were a tease."

His jaw dropped. "What?"

"You owe my brother? I owe him, too. He kept me sane and safe for most of my life. But you know what I'm not going to do?" And now she was walking. More like angrily stomping toward the truck. "I'm not going to let him tell me who I can and can't make love with. Because that's *my* decision. Not his. Just. Mine."

She hopped into the truck. Slammed the door.

Jasper blew out a slow breath. When the lady was angry, she was gorgeous. That flush in her cheeks. The flash of her eyes...*gorgeous*. He hurried to the driver's side, jumped in the vehicle. "It isn't like—"

"Don't kiss me like you can't breathe without me."

He had kissed her that way. No, more as if she *was* the breath he needed. He'd never been so desperate to taste a woman before.

"Don't do that," she snapped at him, "then in the next minute, go all cool and wooden on me. I'm not like you, okay? I don't have a line of partners behind me. I don't play games, and I don't—"

His fingers curled around the steering wheel. "A line of partners?" Jasper repeated in a choked voice. How did she keep surprising him?

The icy chips of her eyes could have cut a lesser

man. "Don't play with me. *That's* what I'm saying. If you want me, then it's about me and you. Not my brother. Not what you owe him or what he owes you."

Because Jasper had saved Cale, too. Not in a jungle, in a desert, when a mine had gone off and they'd both come close to being blown to hell.

"Just crank the truck, Jasper." Now she sounded disgusted. "Maybe we'll both figure out just what it is that we want."

He didn't have to figure it out. He already knew exactly what he wanted. But taking it could prove dangerous.

To him. And to her.

WHEN THE TRUCK stopped in front of the ranch, Veronica pretty much leaped out of the vehicle. She was embarrassed and angry and scared. A combination that had her stomach knotting. She was attracted to Jasper. He seemed attracted to her. But then he'd gone all Ice Man on her and—

The alarm wasn't beeping.

Veronica tensed. She'd unlocked the front door, and, normally, the alarm would beep until she typed in the code.

But the alarm wasn't beeping.

Jasper's arm closed around her shoulder. "What's wrong?"

"The alarm…"

He swore, seeming to realize what *wasn't* happening instantly. Then he was pulling her back. Putting his body in front of hers. He reached for his gun.

She wished she had a weapon, too. Veronica hated feeling helpless. And she was pretty much feeling that way 24/7 these days.

He stepped inside the house. Veronica peered over his shoulder. The foyer looked fine. The den didn't appear disturbed. Maybe it was nothing. A glitch with the alarm.

"Stay here," he said and eased inside the house.

Stay there—out in the open? Um, she hadn't been worried when she'd hopped out of the truck and started walking earlier, but the memory of standing in front of that sheriff's station, waiting—and then seeing two men get shot right before her eyes—that memory was front and center for her. With the silence of her alarm, the security she felt at the ranch had been shattered. The place didn't feel safe.

As for staying out on that porch…

*No, thank you.*

She glanced around. Her gaze searched the small scattering of buildings around the main house. What if a shooter was out there? She'd make a perfect target.

Veronica rushed inside the house and nearly slammed into Jasper. "I'm coming with you," she whispered.

He frowned, but nodded.

They made their way down the hallway. Nothing was missing. Nothing broken. It didn't look as if anyone had been there. Maybe she was wrong.

He motioned with his hand to indicate that they should head up the stairs.

Her fingers curled over the wooden bannister. The third stair creaked beneath her feet, and that sound was far too loud.

Her breathing was too loud, too. Too quick. Too raspy.

He turned at the top of the stairs and headed for her brother's room. The door was partially open. With his left hand, Jasper opened the door wider, even as his right hand kept his gun ready.

The door swung open.

*Destruction.*

The room had been ripped apart. The mattresses slashed. Every dresser and chest drawer yanked out and overturned. The dresser mirror lay in what looked like a thousand pieces.

"Somebody was looking for something." Jasper's quiet voice.

It looked as if somebody had been looking to wreck the place.

Jasper's hand wrapped around her wrist and they headed back into the hallway. The next room they checked was hers.

The door was shut. She was the one to turn the handle and push the door open.

Her room looked even worse. Because it wasn't just her mattresses that were slashed. Her clothes were slashed. Her photos. Every memento that she'd ever had was in pieces on her floor.

It was as if someone had grabbed her and punched her in the face.

This? This was someone looking for something? No, this was a personal attack.

She must have made some kind of faint sound because Jasper's gaze jumped to her face. In that stare, she saw a white-hot fury. It was a fury she felt, too.

*My home. My safe place.*

Someone had come in here and tried to destroy her world. To rip away her safety.

No, to cut away that safety. Because it sure looked as though someone had used a knife on her mattress and clothing.

A knife... The intruder had attacked all of the things that were personal to her. If she'd been there, what would the intruder have done?

Would he have attacked her?

Killed her?

She heard a faint creak. The same creak she'd made when she stepped on the loose stair. In an instant, Jasper was rushing past her and heading for the stairs. "Stop, you son of a—" Jasper yelled, but then his yell died away.

Veronica was right on his heels. She could see why he'd stopped his order. Because the man on the stairs had a gun, too. One that was trembling, but still aimed right up at Jasper.

And that man was Deputy Jimmy Jones.

# Chapter Six

"Drop your weapon!" Jimmy ordered, his voice breaking.

Jasper swore. The last thing he wanted to do was lower his gun. "Tell me why you're in the house."

Jimmy blinked his eyes, eyes that looked watery, nervous. The kid's gun began to lower. "The...front door was open. With...with all the stuff that's been goin' on around here, I was worried." Then his gun flew back up, as if he'd just realized that he'd lowered his hand. "I told you, drop the weapon!"

Jasper lowered his weapon, but he also made sure that he closed the distance between him and Jimmy. If it came down to it, he could still take the deputy out, weapon or no weapon. Close-contact fighting was a specialty for him.

But as soon as Jasper lowered his weapon, Jimmy holstered his own gun. Jimmy's gaze darted to Veronica's face. "Is everything okay?"

"No." Her voice wasn't weak. It was angry. She

gritted, "Someone's been in the house. Cale's room is trashed. So is mine."

But Jasper wasn't so sure it was just about trashing. Sometimes a smart thief could trash the place in order to hide the fact that he'd taken something.

Something very important.

And not even something that had been in Veronica's or Jasper's room. Maybe trashing those particular rooms drew attention away from the fact that he'd taken something small from the rest of the house.

Jasper's gaze swept over the edge of the staircase.

*What did you want?*

"I'll call the sheriff," Jimmy said. "He sent me out here to check on you. He was worried, after what happened last night." Jasper's gaze returned to the deputy just in time to see Jimmy's Adam's apple bob. "Guess he was right to be worried."

*Yeah, he was.*

"I need to finish searching the house," Jasper said.

Jimmy's eyes bulged. "I should do that. I should—"

"You keep an eye on Veronica. That's the most important thing."

Jimmy nodded at once. "Right." His shoulders straightened as his hand went to the holster of his gun.

Hell, what was the kid? Barely twenty? So eager to follow every order. If the kid wasn't careful, he'd get hurt.

Especially with that shaky trigger finger of his.

Jasper turned and headed back up the stairs. His fingers brushed over Veronica's arm. She stiffened at his touch. "I'll be right back," he promised.

She gave a quick nod.

He searched the rest of the rooms upstairs. Heard Jimmy's voice, calling the sheriff. He opened more doors. Nothing looked disturbed in the other rooms, but then, that would be the point, wouldn't it? To focus attention in one spot, while the real action happened someplace else.

*What were you looking for?*

And, more important, had the intruder found what he wanted?

He went back downstairs. Veronica and Jimmy were sitting on the couch. In short work, Jasper checked out the rest of the house. Clear. No more damage.

But what about the buildings close by? Could the intruder be there?

He headed for the front door.

Veronica jumped into his path. "Where are you going?"

He wouldn't sugarcoat this. "It's possible he's still here. There are over a dozen places to hide just outside this door." All of the old buildings. The small stable. "I need to make sure the area's secure."

"Should I...should I do that?" Jimmy asked. His shoulders weren't quite so straight.

The kid looked as if he would faint if Jasper said yes. So, instead, Jasper growled, "No."

Jimmy nodded quickly. "Right, I need to keep Veronica safe."

Her lips compressed. Then she snapped, "If someone would just give me a gun, I'm pretty sure I could keep myself safe."

Jimmy's fingers eased toward his weapon.

Jasper focused on Veronica. "Try to think about what you and Cale have here that someone would want."

She blinked.

"Something that a person would be willing to risk a hell of a lot to get." Because he and Veronica could have come back at any time. The intruder would have needed to watch the house. Watch closely, to see when they left the property.

*Were you here this morning? Were you watching us?*

Jasper headed onto the porch. He kept his body in cover as much as he could as he headed around the area and into the outer buildings. The horses neighed when he got close to them, and they shifted toward him. Jasper gave them a quick pat, but kept moving. His gaze was on the floor, then the small set of stairs that led to the top of the stable.

He climbed the stairs. More hay. Only the hay was scattered near the window. As if someone had tried to clear a space in that area.

Carefully, Jasper moved toward the window. He glanced through it—and had a perfect view of the ranch house and the drive leading up to the home.

Hell.

Their watcher had been close, all right. Jasper couldn't help wondering...*just how long has someone been watching Veronica?*

THE SHERIFF HAD arrived, racing up to the scene with his sirens blaring. Wyatt was in the house now with Veronica and Jimmy, and despite his search, Jasper hadn't found any other signs of the watcher.

Making sure that he was a safe distance away from the house—the last thing Jasper wanted was to be overheard—he pulled out his phone and made a quick call to Logan. He briefed the team leader on the situation, a situation that had him clenching the phone in his fist, and then Jasper growled, "I don't like this setup."

Logan's sigh carried easily over the phone. "I know you don't, but what options do we have?"

He could think of a few, starting with... "I take Veronica out of here. I get her someplace safe."

"You know her brother. Is there any place that guy wouldn't be able to track?"

Hell, no. That was the problem. Cale was deadly. Fierce. A tracker who was almost as good as Gunner. But there was an important point Logan needed to get. "I don't think this attack came from her brother," Jasper said, voice tight. "He wouldn't trash his own place. Wouldn't slice his sister's clothes and destroy the things that mattered most to her." That wasn't Cale.

"You sure about that?" Logan asked softly. "You know what the psych report said."

The psych report. Right. The one that Uncle Sam kept shoving down their throats. When Cale had left the Rangers, the EOD had thought about recruiting him. Only a psych report had surfaced. One that said Cale's tendency for extreme violence couldn't be controlled. That Cale Lane was a menace to himself, and others.

That he had serious aggressive tendencies that could result in harm to even those close to him.

But on this point, Jasper didn't think his instincts were wrong. "Cale wouldn't have to search the house. If he'd hidden something there, he'd just slip in and get it, not leave that mess for his sister to find." That would be the last thing he'd do. "No, it's someone else." Someone they hadn't counted on. And if there were more players in the game... "I don't think Cale was behind the attempted kidnapping."

Silence from the other end of the phone.

"Cale wouldn't need two men to force his sister in a car." With her history, Jasper knew that Cale would never have been behind anyone forcing her off the road. "If he wanted to get Veronica alone, all he'd have to do would be to call her, and she'd go anyplace he told her to go." Which was a scary proposition. "We're still monitoring all her calls, right?" he couldn't help asking.

"Yes, we are."

Somewhat reassuring.

"Someone wanted to get control of Veronica for the same reason that we wanted to approach her." Before he smashed the phone, he forced his fingers to ease their grip. "Someone else wants to use her against Cale."

"The man probably has a whole lot of enemies."

The kind who wouldn't mind torturing an innocent woman to get what they wanted.

*They want you, Cale.*

"We need extra surveillance out here," Jasper snapped. The idea of Veronica being watched by someone, of her being targeted, had rage twisting in his gut. "I want fingerprints taken from the house. I want to know just who the hell is playing with us."

Who'd tried to hurt Veronica.

"A team is on the way now. They'll search for prints, but do you know what was taken?"

Jasper glanced back at the house. "I'll find out." He paused. "*If* the intruder found what he wanted." All those slashes and the destruction upstairs... maybe that had happened after the intruder didn't find what he wanted. Whoever it was could have been furious. Enraged. So he took out that fury on Cale and Veronica. "I don't like this," Jasper gritted.

"I know." Logan's voice was softer, and Jasper knew that Logan really did understand. On their last big mission, the woman Logan loved—*had loved, for years*—had been put in a killer's deadly path. She'd been bait, and the killer had come far too close to taking out both Juliana and Logan.

Logan's gaze had been haunted for weeks after the attack. He'd realized just how close he'd come to losing his Juliana, and he'd been afraid.

If anyone could relate, it would be Logan. Sighing, Jasper said, "I don't want her put at risk."

"The ranch covers a huge area. Her nearest neighbor is over forty miles away."

Yeah, and the ranch was overgrown, with extra buildings scattered around and far too many places for anyone to hide.

"It'll be tough to keep every section clear," Logan added.

Tough, but not impossible. "I'll take Veronica with me. We'll start searching the north end of the property."

"And I'll send a team to begin in the south."

Because their watcher might not have left entirely. He could easily still be killing close.

*You won't get her.*

"Jasper." There was a tense note in Logan's voice. "Is this case getting personal?"

It wasn't supposed to be. He'd already been screened. Checked to make sure that the bonds he'd had with Cale wouldn't get in the way of performing the mission. But when the team leader asked about the mission getting personal, Jasper knew that Logan wasn't referring to the other ex-ranger.

*Veronica.* "I can do the job," Jasper said, deliberately not answering. Sure, he wanted Veronica, pretty damn desperately, but he couldn't be falling for the woman, not that fast. Lust wasn't personal. Lust was just about need. "I've got this."

"That's what I thought, too. Then when I realized how much danger was right beside Juliana, I wanted to kill everyone who ever *thought* about hurting her."

*That's how I feel.* "I'm in control" was Jasper's response.

Then the screen door opened. Veronica appeared on the porch. She looked tired. Her eyes were big, but dark shadows whispered under them.

"Send out the crew," Jasper said, and ended the call. He shoved the phone into his back pocket. He'd gotten a holster from his truck and it was under the edge of the light jacket he wore. The heat had cooled, giving way to the dark clouds and the storms that the forecasters said would continue soon.

Not that he really needed the jacket for anything more than covering his weapon.

"What crew is coming?" Veronica asked him.

Then she held up her hand. "No, wait, let me guess, your federal buddies? They're coming to my house?"

"You think the sheriff's going to sweep for prints?" he asked her.

"No." Her hand dropped. "But they will?"

"They already have a tech team at Last Chance. Logan and Gunner...those guys are in my debt, Veronica. They can do this job for me. Hell, it's the least they can do. Someone wants something that your brother—or even you—have, and there's no telling how far that person will go to get what he wants."

Her steps were slow as she eased off the porch and came toward him. He was positioned with his truck in front of him and the house behind him. Good cover, for the moment. She advanced until less than a foot separated them. "You think...you think this was just about finding something I have?"

Yeah, he did.

"But m-my clothes..." Her lips trembled. "All of the things in my room. There was so much fury in there. So much hate." She raked a hand through her hair. "How'd he get in? How'd he get past my alarm?"

"If you know what you're doing, it's easy enough to bypass most alarms." With the right tools. Unless, of course, the intruder had already known the code for her system. Then all he would have needed to do was type in the digits. Didn't get simpler than that.

"You told Wyatt a few minutes ago…" Her gaze darted to the stables. "You said someone was watching me?"

Jasper nodded.

She crept even closer. The wind blew the scent of honeysuckles toward him. He stiffened, aware that this wasn't the time to get turned on by her.

But then, he seemed to get turned on every time he looked at her.

"I've felt like someone was watching me for a while now." Her confession was stark.

The breath hissed between his teeth. "Why didn't you tell me?"

"I told the sheriff." Her shoulders rolled. "He came out and checked a few times, but didn't see anything. I thought…I thought I was just being paranoid."

Paranoid, his as—

"It started about two months ago. I don't even know what made me nervous at first." Her gaze was on the stable. "The horses…I think it was them… they seemed agitated one day. I heard them neighing and pushing at their stalls. I went out to check, but nothing was wrong."

Or the watcher had just slipped away before she'd gotten to the stables.

Because he needed to know just how often the watcher could have been around, Jasper asked, "Do you just feel like you're being watched at the ranch?"

She shook her head, glanced back at him. "I felt that way in town once or twice. I'd hear footsteps, look over my shoulder, but no one would be there." Her shoulders hunched. "You really think that some-one's been watching me this long? I haven't just been imagining it?"

He knew his eyes said that, yes, he thought that. "Why?"

"Because maybe you aren't the only one look-ing for Cale." Not even close. "Maybe the others think you're their key to finding him." That was what the EOD had thought. That Cale would never completely leave his sister. He'd come back for her, sooner rather than later. "You are his only living relative."

"They want to…use me against him?"

He nodded. "Looks that way." The words were stilted. *I'm using you.*

"Cale's done something…bad."

Serious understatement. She sounded almost like a lost child, but maybe that was the point. She saw Cale as the big, protective older brother. Perfect. Strong.

Now she was starting to wonder about his flaws.

"Think about this," he urged her. "What would someone want to find in that house? Did Cale keep anything special there? You said you went through his computer before."

"His computer wasn't touched."

How was she so sure?

"I, um, put a special security system on it. Trust me on this, no one will be getting past that."

If not the computer, then what would Cale have? Why suddenly get so desperate to find it? If the watcher had been eyeing the house for months, then the guy could have broken in anytime.

But he'd chosen that specific day. Chosen a time hours after Reed Montgomery was killed.

"Veronica!"

She turned at the sheriff's call. He hurried down the front steps, a worried frown pulling his brows low. "Veronica, those feds just called me. They're sending a team out here." He gave her a fierce stare. "I don't know how long it will take them to sweep for prints, but I just… I don't think you should be staying out here by yourself. Not with these murders going on."

Murders that were shattering the peace of Whiskey Ridge.

"There's only one motel in town," she said, lips curving in a smile that was sad. "If I leave my house, don't you think anyone watching me would realize exactly where I'd gone?"

"You can stay with me," Wyatt offered at once.

Jasper stiffened. He didn't like the way he'd caught the sheriff staring at Veronica. A guy knew lust when he saw it. The sheriff wasn't about to get cozy with Veronica.

Jasper knew the jealousy for exactly what it was. *Stay away from her.* He glared the message at the sheriff.

Only the sheriff wasn't looking at him. His total focus was on Veronica. "You don't need to be alone," Wyatt continued, and that was when Jasper realized that the sheriff's voice was a little too intense. Emotions hummed beneath the surface. "You shouldn't be alone. I can—"

"She's not alone," Jasper growled. Then, when Wyatt glanced over at him, Jasper offered the sheriff a tiger's smile. "I'm standing right here."

The sheriff narrowed his eyes. When he spoke, his voice was clipped now. Not filled with warm emotion. Biting with fury. "I did some checking on you. Sure, you got bureau friends, but I know about *you.*"

No, the sheriff knew what his fake bio said. The bio that Sydney had put in place for him.

"You've been to every hellhole on earth, and you left a trail of bullets and bodies behind you."

"I was following orders," Jasper said, his own anger rousing. The guy was trying to attack him? Trying to make Veronica doubt him? "Sometimes orders aren't pretty."

"Yes, but that was when you were in the military. Years ago. You've been in bar fights, brawls. You've—"

He wanted to get in a good, hard fight right now with the sheriff.

"—got connections with some shady characters who have spent most of their lives in jail." The sheriff turned his gaze back to Veronica. "I don't think you should trust him. You *know* me. I can help you."

Damn it. The last thing he needed was this guy trying to play white knight.

Or trying to get in Veronica's bed.

*Back off, Wyatt. Back. Off.* Jasper's hands clenched into fists.

Veronica cast a fast glance at Jasper, then turned back to the sheriff. "When I needed help, Jasper was the first person to listen to me. The first to agree that he'd try and find Cale." Veronica shook her head. "I begged you for months, Wyatt, but you wouldn't even fill out a missing person's report."

"Because Cale was supposed to be on a mission—"

"I trust Jasper."

Damn straight. He flashed another hard smile at the sheriff.

Wyatt's glittering gaze met his. "I don't. Check your timeline, Ronnie. He comes to town, and folks start dying. He comes to town, and your place gets trashed."

"I was *with* him then."

"Maybe he has a partner. Maybe he has—"

The sheriff was accusing him? Jasper stepped forward. "Get some facts to back up any accusations you're making."

Veronica pushed between the men. "Calm down, both of you." Her breath expelled in a rush. "Wyatt, Jasper may have shady friends, but so do you. So does Cale. I've seen them. Heck, I told you that I'd been going through old photos of his and just the pictures of some of those guys intimidated me." Guys like Reed Montgomery. She paused, then said, "He may have some dangerous friends, but Jasper also has some friends who are coming in very handy." She tilted her head and studied the sheriff. "If he was involved in this, would he be pulling in the feds? Jasper is helping us, getting more done than—"

*You.*

She didn't finish her sentence. Maybe she didn't have to.

Veronica touched the sheriff's shoulder. "I'm sorry, but I trust Jasper."

"What if you're making a mistake?" Wyatt asked her, voice raw.

"I don't know." She didn't look at Jasper when she whispered this confession.

Jasper put his arm around Veronica's shoulder. He pulled her against his side. The woman seemed to fit him so well. "I'm going to stay with her. I won't let anyone hurt her."

"You'd better not." With that snarl, Wyatt turned away and marched back into the house.

Veronica watched him go.

Jasper wanted to ask her about the sheriff. About the possessive gaze he had swept over her. But now her eyes were on him, and for a second, he didn't say anything at all.

"I have to do something," she said. "I can't just stay here and watch some crime techs go through all my things."

And she couldn't search through the house to see what had been taken, not until Logan's crew arrived. He blew out a slow breath. "Let's search the rest of the property." Well, the north end, for now. "Any buildings or places where someone can hole up for a while." Rain was coming, so they were working against the clock, or rather, the weather. Jasper wanted to get out there and see if there were any fresh tracks before the rain washed those tracks away. But, judging by the gathering clouds, there wasn't gonna be much time.

"You think the person who broke into my house—"

"It's a lot of land. I just want to be sure."

Her lips pressed together as she thought for a moment, and then she said, "I searched the area, went in all the sheds and the two cabins, about a month ago. I didn't see anything then." Her lips pulled down. "That was my third search. I thought that maybe Cale was in one of those places."

*Maybe he is now.* Because Jasper sure thought the man was back in town.

"Let's look again," he murmured. "Sometimes you just need a fresh pair of eyes." Or a trained gaze that was used to seeing what most people missed.

Like the faint signs left by another hunter's presence.

In the distance, thunder rumbled.

He nodded toward the truck. "Let's tell the sheriff where we're heading. If we hurry, we can beat the storm." And catch anyone who might be lingering around, waiting for another moment to strike.

*Not on my watch.*

THERE WASN'T EXACTLY a road that led over the ranch's property. Not a real road, anyway. Dirt and some gravel. If you tried hard, you could almost follow a trail.

Sometimes.

The truck bounced along the path, heaving over the terrain. Veronica tried to shove all the dark images out of her head—not images about her slashed items, but images of Reed Montgomery. His last minutes.

What did her clothes matter compared to what he'd suffered?

"You okay?"

Her head snapped up at Jasper's drawl. "F-fine."

"You seemed to be about a million miles away."

Not nearly that far. Last Chance wasn't nearly that far away. She swallowed. There was a question she wanted to ask, but she wasn't sure how he would react. "Jasper…" She glanced at him from the corner of her eye.

His profile was strong, hard, his attention seemingly all on the area before the truck. His gaze swept over the land, going from left to right, then back again, every few moments.

"What's it like to kill a man?" she asked him.

His stare flew to her. "What?"

There hadn't been an easy way to ask the question. "You've killed. I know it." Just like her brother. "Reed—the man who killed him… I was wondering…"

"Killing in combat is damn well not the same thing as killing in cold blood."

No. "But it's still taking a life."

He growled.

"Does it leave a scar inside?" She couldn't stop herself. "Or do you not feel it at all?" Cale hadn't seemed to feel anything after his missions. Or if he had, he sure hadn't told her about any weakness.

"You asking if it's easy to kill and walk away?"

No. Maybe. She just—

"It's not easy. It's *never* easy. When you're on a mission, you do what has to be done to protect your unit. You take a life to *save* lives. And you don't just forget it the instant the body hits the sand."

The sand?

"You don't forget the memories. You remember

the smells and the colors and the sights of the land around you. You remember your enemy's scent. The way he looked when he fell. The way the blood felt on your hands if you were close." His words were fast and hard, hitting like bullets in the car. "If you kill from a distance, it's not better. You hear the sounds of the shots. The last cry a target makes... *You don't forget.* Those images can haunt your dreams."

His fingers tightened around the steering wheel. "A soldier isn't a sociopath. He's no serial killer. He does his job. He protects his country and his team. The serials out there, the killers who walk the streets...I don't know what the hell they think or feel. I'm not even sure they *do* feel."

His answer wasn't what she'd expected. Not necessarily what she'd hoped to hear. She knew why Cale had left the army. Knew about the psych evaluation gone wrong.

*What category does Cale belong to...soldier? Sociopath?*

She'd hoped that by listening to Jasper, a man who'd been through so many of the same experiences that had marked her brother, she'd—

What? Veronica rubbed her forehead. That she'd understand the killer better? Understand Cale?

Understand the dark and dangerous man beside her?

Sighing, Veronica said, "I didn't ask to upset you."

"Why did you ask?"

"To understand you."

"Is understanding me that important to you?"

"Yes." Simple.

Silence then.

She waited, not speaking again, just listening to the roll of thunder. The storm was coming closer. Leaning forward, Veronica stared up through the windshield. The sky looked almost black. "I'm not sure how much longer this storm's gonna hold off."

Not long enough for them to get back to the main house, that was for sure. And trying to drive over this faint path in a strong storm… A shiver slid over her. After her recent attack on the road, she sure wasn't eager for another crash.

"How much longer until we reach the cabin?" Jasper asked her.

"About five minutes. Maybe ten. Keep going straight, turn right when you see the stream." Her hands were flat against the dashboard. She pushed herself back, feeling the seat belt pull over her shoulder.

"I'm not your brother."

Veronica was so shocked by his words that she almost forgot the impending storm. "I never thought you were." If she had, then she sure wouldn't have made out with him.

"The things I do…what I feel…*that's me.*"

*Uh, okay.*

"I grew up in the system, too. Became an army ranger just like him, so maybe you think that somehow makes—"

"The system?" She cut across his words, straightening. "You mean the foster-care system?"

A quick nod.

"I didn't know that. Cale never told me."

"Not really much to tell. Thousands of kids hit the system every year." A shrug. "I was one of them." His gaze was searching the area before them once more.

"Did your parents die, too?" She could understand his loss. The pain he'd felt when they'd died.

"They didn't die. They just didn't want me."

Instinctively, she shook her head. "No, I'm sure that's not—"

"My dad split when he found out my mom was pregnant. My mother kept me for a couple of years, just long enough to realize that she didn't want to be stuck with a kid. Then she dumped me in the waiting room of a local hospital."

She wanted to touch him, to comfort him. There was no emotion in his voice, but she could feel his pain.

"I never saw her again," he said. His knuckles were white around the wheel.

"Did you want to?" Dumb question. Surely, he'd dreamed of his mother coming back.

"No. I never wanted to see her again. The only thing she ever did was hit me and yell at me. I was glad to be free." His gaze flashed over to her.

She held his gaze for a moment, then he glanced back at the road.

It was her turn to talk then. "Maybe you think you know me, because you've heard bits and pieces of my life over the years. But I'm more than just Cale's little sister. More than just the woman who stutters in the corner and—"

"Your stutter's sexy." A hard pause. "And if anyone tried to put you in a corner, I'd kick their ass."

Oh. She glanced toward the windshield. The rain was coming down in hard pellets now. So much for beating the storm. "T-turn right." The stutter didn't embarrass her now. But her cheeks still glowed.

The truck slowed, turned. A few minutes later, the cabin was in sight.

More thunder rumbled, and when she climbed out of the truck, lightning flashed across the sky. The drops of rain beat against her skin, growing harder with every step she took.

Jasper had his gun out. He paused on the old, slightly sagging porch, and glanced at her. The droplets of rain clung to his skin. "Stay behind me when we go inside."

Because he thought the watcher might be there? Or because he thought her brother could be inside?

*Trust him.*

Veronica nodded. Then Jasper pushed open the door and rushed inside the darkness.

## Chapter Seven

The cabin was deserted. Jasper checked every closet, checked under the bed and even did a scan of the outside perimeter.

Their watcher wasn't there. Neither was Cale.

But there was no dust inside the place. The bed was made, and some canned goods were even stocked in the small kitchen. Someone *could* have been there, and that someone could have covered his tracks pretty well.

The generator hadn't been turned on, but that would have been a dead giveaway to someone else's presence in the cabin. Since he wasn't trying to hide his presence, Jasper flipped on that generator. The lights flashed, and he saw Veronica rubbing her arms.

He picked up a blanket from the back of the old couch. "Here." His voice was gruff. He'd been too abrupt with her in the truck. But her questions had been like a knife, cutting into old wounds.

*No one wants you, not even your own mother.*

The other kids at his school hadn't wasted much time in making his life hell.

Then when he'd grown older, he'd discovered there were other kinds of hells, especially on the battlefield.

Her fingers curled around the blanket. "Th-thank you."

He ran a hand through his damp hair. The cabin seemed to shake around them with the force of the rattling thunder. "We aren't getting back to the main house tonight."

She shook her head. "I don't want to try and drive through this."

He didn't want to push her right into one of her nightmares. He reached for his phone, called the sheriff. "It's Jasper." The sheriff immediately started asking questions, all about Veronica. *Back off, man.* Yeah, it was pretty obvious the guy was sweet on Veronica.

Jasper glanced over at her.

*So am I.* A complication he sure hadn't counted on when he'd signed up for the mission.

"We're staying at the cabin on the north end of the property. No, no," Jasper said, when the sheriff tried to interrupt, "we aren't coming back tonight. We'll check in tomorrow, once the storm has blown past us." He ended the call over the sheriff's objections.

Jasper stared at Veronica a moment, then asked, "Is he always like that?"

She looked over her shoulder at him. Her wet hair
was a dark mass around her neck. "Like what?"

"He doesn't want you out of his sight."

*I understand how that feels.*

Veronica shrugged. "He's protective of everyone
in Whiskey Ridge."

What? Of all two hundred folks scattered around?

Jasper began to stalk toward her. His fingers were
itching to touch the softness of her skin. No, he just
wanted to touch *her.* "It's different," he said. "I can
see it in his eyes." And it made him…jealous. He
knew the bitter taste—he'd felt it before. Too often.

*Jealous of the kids with real homes, real families.*

"He wants you," Jasper said flatly.

Her lashes lifted and she met his gaze.

"The question is…" *Don't touch her, not yet.* The
rain pounded down outside, tapping hard against the
old tin roof. "Do you want him?" If she did, he'd
back off. Because he wasn't going to—

"Are you really that blind?" she asked him with a
shake of her head and a faint smile. "Can't you tell
that you're the one I want?"

She was the one he was desperate to have.

They were alone. Sheltered from the storm. No
interruptions. No danger.

Just…

Them.

His fingers rose, traced the soft curve of her
cheek. Slid down, down, and then he was cupping

her chin, tilting her head back. He tasted the lingering raindrops on her lips.

Just the touch of her lips against his sent a powerful wave of desire pulsing through his body. The kiss started gentle. She deserved gentle. She was delicate and warm and *everything* he wanted.

But it was hard to stay gentle when he wanted her so badly that his hands were starting to shake. His arousal pressed against the front of his jeans. Heavy, hard, aching—for her.

"Don't be a tease this time," she whispered. "If you want me, it's just about me. Not about owing anyone anything. Just me. Just you." The blanket fell from her shoulders. Veronica's arms rose and wrapped around him. She pulled him closer, and closer was exactly where he wanted to be.

*Just me. Just you.*

The kiss became deeper. Hotter. He forgot about the chill from the rain, because the woman was burning him up. Her soft fingers pushed up his shirt.

Jasper was only too eager to toss that shirt across the room. Then his hands went to her shirt.

*Go easy. Go easy.* The mantra was repeating in his head.

"You don't have to," she whispered.

He frowned at her. What was she saying?

"I like you anyway—you don't have to be easy for me."

The mantra hadn't just been in his head, and the woman was about to *shred* his control.

He lifted her shirt, carefully, then tossed it to the floor. She wore a black bra, one that wasn't covered in lace, but was just as incredibly sexy as it pushed up her beautiful breasts.

He stared at her a moment, savoring the view, and then he had to touch that tempting flesh.

Her bra hit the floor.

His fingers curled around her breasts. Veronica gasped and arched toward him. Her nails bit into his arms. He liked that bite.

A lot.

He lifted her into the air, carrying her easily.

"Jasper?"

Five steps, and he had her at the bed. He lowered her onto the covers. The mattress squeaked beneath them. The rain kept falling. The thunder echoed across the sky.

He pressed a kiss to her breast. Stroked her with his hands and he loved the way that she arched into his touch. Her breasts were so sensitive, and they tasted so damn sweet.

While he kissed her flesh, his hand slid down between their bodies. Her shoes were gone, kicked away, and he wanted her jeans gone, too. He'd fantasized about having her naked beneath him, and that fantasy was about to become all too real.

As long as his control would last.

He wanted to *devour* her. Jasper couldn't ever remember wanting a woman so badly. His heart raced, a drumbeat that shook his chest and echoed in his ears.

His fingers pulled down her zipper, yanked open the snap. Then his fingers were pushing inside that opening, and caressing her through the thin silk of her panties. His eyes locked on her face, on the pleasure that whispered over her beautiful features. Her eyes had gone even brighter with that pleasure.

She was warm and soft beneath the silk. He couldn't tell where the silk ended and she began.

"Jasper, I *need* you."

He was desperate for her.

She lifted her hips, shoved down her jeans. He pulled away from her, only long enough to ditch the rest of his own clothes and grab the protection that he'd—optimistically—put in his wallet earlier.

In seconds, he was back, pushing his body between her legs, letting his hands and mouth caress her flesh and loving the soft moans that spilled from her mouth. He wanted her ready for him, wanted to make this as good for her as he possibly could.

*It has to be good. She has to want me.*

He positioned his aroused flesh at the entrance of her body. His fingers twined with hers, and he pushed her hands back against the bed. Then, slowly—*will keep my control, will keep*—he began to push into her.

And realized, very, very quickly, just what she'd meant when she'd told him that she didn't have a line of partners as he did.

Because she hadn't been with *any* other partners.

Jasper froze, even as every instinct he possessed demanded that he take her. That he thrust forward and claim the pleasure that waited. "Veronica?"

Her legs wrapped around his hips and she pushed toward him. "Why are you stopping?"

"Because I don't want to hurt you." He growled the stark truth.

Her bright gaze held his. There was so much trust in her stare. "You won't. I want you."

He thrust into her. She gasped, and he was worried it was from pain, but then she was smiling at him, a smile that made his chest ache, and she met his thrusts, holding him tight, moving in perfect rhythm with him. Faster and faster.

The tension built within him, but no way was he going to find release without ensuring Veronica's pleasure. He shifted positions slightly, making sure that the angle of his thrusts would press his flesh against the most sensitive part of Veronica's body.

Again and again, he drove into her.

He kissed her, tasting her need and desire. His fingers were still locked with hers.

Her sex clenched around him. Her body tensed. Then she was pressing up harder, driving for the release that was so close for them both.

His control began to crack.

The thrusts were deeper, wilder.

The ripples of her release squeezed around his flesh. Nothing had ever felt so good. Nothing—

Then his own pleasure hit him, swamping out every other thought and sending him crashing into a climax so intense that the world fell away for an instant.

There was only Veronica.

Soft flesh.

Sweet taste.

Only him holding her, still thrusting into her.

His mouth lifted from hers. Their eyes held. He looked into her gaze, and realized he was looking at the one thing he'd always wanted.

And the one thing that fate just might try to take away from him.

*Want her. Need her.*

No matter what happened in the coming days, he'd fight like hell to keep her with him.

THE STORM KEPT him away. He knew that Jasper had gone out searching for him. Knew that Jasper and Veronica were holed up in the cabin.

He could try to get to them now, but he'd have to battle the rain and the wind and the lightning that had already hit two trees. The storm would mute the sounds of his approach, but he wouldn't be able to fire on them in this weather. He'd have to go in, fight hand to hand against them both.

He didn't want to tangle with Jasper, not with bare hands. But using bullets? That was a whole different story.

His fingers curled over the gun that he kept with him. He'd found his own shelter. He would stay there, until the storm was gone. Then he'd use his weapon. He'd find Jasper and Veronica.

*You won't mess this up for me. I worked too hard.*

He knew exactly where they were—his advantage. He could pick off Jasper, take out the man with just a squeeze of his trigger finger.

*One down, one to go.*

So easy. All he had to do was wait.

The storm wouldn't last forever. It never did.

Just. Wait.

Good thing he was a patient man, and one hell of a fine shot.


"Why?" Jasper's rumbling voice pulled Veronica from the light sleep that she'd slipped into for just a few moments.

She blinked, turned and found Jasper staring down at her. She smiled up at him, still feeling too good to let any inhibitions cloud her moment.

"You waited twenty-eight years to take a lover," Jasper pressed. "Why the hell did you choose me?"

"How did you know I was twenty-eight?"

He growled. "Your brother must have told me your birthday."

Her smile stretched a bit. He sure sounded stressed. But as for the waiting part... That was easy. "Because I've got good taste?"

He blinked at her. "You what?"

She laughed then, unable to help herself. "I wanted you, Jasper. There's no big mystery there. I wanted you. I chose you." As simple as that. Or, actually, maybe it was more complicated, but she didn't want to examine her feelings too deeply just now. Couldn't they just talk about desire?

Men and women wanted each other every day. They made love every day. Why were she and Jasper so different from everyone else?

*We aren't.*

Just a man. And a woman.

Her fingers slid over his chest. Over the scars that crisscrossed his flesh. So much pain. So many battles. When she thought of all he'd endured, it made her heart ache.

His muscles were rock-hard beneath her touch. His flesh was so hot that her fingers almost felt singed. And, of course, she was drawn to the fire.

She rose and pressed a kiss to the slanting scar on his shoulder. He stiffened. She pressed another kiss to the jagged scar too close to his heart. One to the long scar that sliced across his stomach. With every kiss, he seemed to become even more tense.

"Why do you risk your life so much?" she asked quietly as she feathered another kiss over a scar that whispered of his pain. *What are you trying to prove?* But she wouldn't ask that question. She'd already asked him enough questions that hurt.

His fingers curled around her arms. "Don't."

Was he telling her to stop kissing him? Or stop trying to know the man he was, beneath the scars and that sexy grin?

"You deserved better," he gritted.

She shook her head and said what she knew to be true. "There isn't anyone better than you."

In a flash, she found herself on her back, crushed into the soft covers, with a very fierce Jasper over her. "You break through my control."

Her heart raced as she held his gaze. "You don't need control with me."

"Yes." Ragged. "I need it more with you than with anyone else."

The words didn't frighten her, but they did turn her on.

"Can you take me again?" he asked, desire darkening his eyes.

"Try to stop me," she whispered. Yes, she'd been a virgin, but she wasn't about to pretend shyness with him. When she'd been growing up, most guys hadn't looked at her twice. She truly had been the stuttering girl in the corner, the girl with no confidence and old clothes. Then when she'd gotten older, she just hadn't been interested in playing games with lovers who didn't care about her.

She hadn't been interested, until Jasper. He was different. He cared. She trusted him.

*He is different.*

Maybe he was just the guy she'd always been looking for. Someone to hold her in a storm. To laugh with her in the sunlight. To even love her?

He took care of the protection—he must have been a Boy Scout—then he was pushing into her with a long, slow surge of his hips. Her body quickened beneath him, her heart racing, breasts tightening, sex aching. Pleasure still pulsed through her, and every move of his hips had her already sensitive body yearning more for him.

It wasn't a slow rise to release this time. His thrusts came harder. Wilder. Deeper.

She felt him along every inch of her flesh, as if he were trying to imprint himself on her body.

The bed shook beneath them. He drove into her, pushing with a leashed ferocity. She met that ferocity, took everything that he had and demanded more.

Because she wasn't going to settle for less than taking everything that he had to give.

When the climax hit, it seemed to explode over them both at the same time. She held tightly to him, curling her arms around him, and he held just as tightly to her. She could feel the frantic race of his heart—or was that hers? Then she realized it didn't matter. Nothing mattered in that moment....

Just pleasure.

Just him.

GUNNER ORTEZ SWORE when the lightning hit the tree beside him, coming far too close for his peace of mind.

"Hurry inside!" Sydney yelled from the entrance of the small shack they'd stumbled across moments before.

The ground was soaked, gutted, and their SUV had gotten stuck in the sludge. With the sky opening up above them and the deluge battering down upon them, they'd been lucky to find this dry spot.

He brushed by her, heading inside the small area.

The wind howled behind him, and he turned, shoving the door closed.

Sydney's footsteps shuffled softly by him in the dark. Then he heard the scratch of a match. Light flared, too brief, too small, but then Sydney was lifting a lantern and the light grew stronger.

There were blankets on the floor of the shack. A few more lanterns.

"Looks like we aren't the only ones who found this place," Sydney murmured as her gaze swept around the room, lingering in the corners—in the dark shadows.

He tensed and automatically reached for his

weapon, but the other visitor—whoever it had been—was gone.

*For now.*

"We'll stay alert," Gunner said with a nod, "just in case he comes back." Because while Gunner knew he was one of the best trackers working for Uncle Sam, even he wasn't much good in a storm like this. All footprints and broken branches that would normally mark a person's passage would be gone, thanks to the rain and the wind.

The storm would provide the perfect cover for Cale Lane.

*But you won't catch me unaware.*

Because Gunner had one motto…*never let down your guard.*

Sydney walked closer to him.

Why couldn't he seem to apply his motto to her?

Her hair was wet—they'd both gotten soaked before finding this place—and she shivered. Immediately, he grabbed for one of the blankets and wrapped it around her shoulders.

Her fingers brushed against his. "Thank you."

He jumped back, moving faster than if she'd shot him. And he'd been shot plenty of times.

Sydney frowned. "Gunner?"

He cleared his throat. "The storm isn't going to be letting up anytime soon." Which meant he and Sydney might have to bunk down for the night.

*A night with Sydney.* Hell. More torture for him.

"Why do you always pull away?"

The quiet question shocked him, so he lied. But, in one way or another, it seemed as if he'd been lying to her for years. "I don't know what you mean, Syd."

She growled. An angry little sound that shouldn't have been sexy. Unfortunately, everything she did seemed sexy to him. That was a big part of his problem.

*Hands off.* But his hands wanted to be...on.

He put as much distance between them as he could. Since the shack was about nine feet long, that wasn't a whole lot of space.

"You know exactly what I mean." Then she started to stalk toward him. "I want a real answer."

She'd put the lantern down, but the light spilled just enough for him to clearly see that her delicate face was set in determination. She closed in on him.

He raised his hands—*have to touch her*—and curled his fingers around her shoulders. "We're working a case. We're partners, that's all."

She stared back up at him. Her lips were full and parted, and he wanted to kiss her.

He'd wanted to kiss her for years.

*She's not yours.* He had to keep reminding himself of that fact. Sydney wasn't meant to be with him. She'd been engaged to his half brother. She and Slade were the ones who should have had the happy ending. The picket fence. That whole picture-perfect dream.

*Not. Me.*

But Slade was dead now. And Sydney was lifting her hand to touch his face. Her fingers rasped over the faint stubble that coated his jaw. "Don't," he gritted out.

"Why not?"

"We're on a mission—"

"And we're alone. We can talk, without anyone else hearing us. Without anyone else watching us." Her hand dropped. He didn't let her go. Maybe he didn't want to. "You almost died on our last case. Do you know how that made me feel?"

He'd cheated death more times than he could count. Unlike Slade. Some nights, Gunner could still hear the echoes of Sydney's cries. He'd had to pull her away from Slade's body. Force her out of that hell of a jungle and get her to safety.

*I lost him, but I damn sure wasn't going to lose her, too.*

She was staring up at him now, waiting for a response, her body a silken temptation. He exhaled slowly. "I'm sure you were worried." Because Sydney worried about everyone. Her heart was too big; she cared too much.

"I wasn't worried," she said immediately, heat in her words. "I was terrified. I don't want anything happening to you."

And he'd die before he'd let anything happen to her. She was the whole reason he was still with the

EOD. The better to keep watch on her. The better to stay close to her.

He was still touching her.

*Hands. Off.* He pulled his hands away, clenched his fists.

"I think about you." Her voice had dropped to a husky whisper. A pause, then, "Do you think about me?"

*Too much.* "Slade." It was an effort to force the name out. Like cutting open a wound that had just started to heal. "You—"

"I don't want to crawl into the ground with him."

He wasn't so sure. Right after he'd brought her back from South America, he'd had to watch her so closely. Then *he'd* been the one to be terrified. But Sydney had healed in the past two years, become stronger and started to look more like the vibrant woman he remembered, and not a ghost.

"I want to live. I want a *life* again."

His heart began to pound too heavily in his chest. What was she saying?

"You saved me that day, and, Gunner, I want to be with you."

She rose onto her toes. Her body pressed against his. Her lips touched his—

He should have pushed her away in that first instant. Gunner *knew* that he should have pushed her away.

He shouldn't have locked his arms around her as if

he was desperate. He shouldn't have held so tightly as if she were his lifeline. He definitely shouldn't have kissed her so wildly—as if he needed her more than anything else.

But he'd never kissed her before. Never been so close to the thing he wanted the most. So he kissed her, he became reckless with his need and didn't pull back. He didn't push her away and tell her that what they were doing was wrong.

Because it felt too right.

His hand slid beneath her hair, tilted her head back. The kiss became deeper.

She trembled against him. Her fingers were over his chest, her right hand over his heart.

He wanted to strip her clothes away. To kiss every inch of her, to claim her.

*She isn't yours to claim.*

The reminder burned through his mind. His head lifted.

"I wanted you to do that," Sydney whispered. "For so long now."

He stiffened. This wasn't hands off. He tried to force his hands to free her.

She shook her head. "You want me. I want you." She rose onto her toes and pressed a quick kiss to his lips. "Why can't we have what we want?"

Because she didn't know the secret guilt that he

carried. If she did, Sydney would never let him close to her again. He didn't answer her, but he did back away.

Her hands fell to her sides. "Will he always be between us?"

The question was like a punch to his gut.

"He's gone, Gunner. As much as that truth hurts us both...*Slade is gone.*"

Because he'd left his brother to die in a jungle, seen him get taken down by gunfire that ripped into Slade's chest. *But I didn't get him out of there. I got Sydney out.*

Slade's grave was a jungle in the middle of Peru. Slade had never come home, not even in death.

"Why is it me?" Gunner rasped the question when he'd meant to remain silent.

Sydney blinked at him as if lost.

But she couldn't be lost. The suspicion that he had ate at his soul. "When you look at me, do you see him?" Was that what she wanted? A substitute for her dead lover?

Her indrawn breath was almost painful to hear. "Bastard."

He was. In every sense of the word.

"I've moved on, Gunner. It tore me apart, but...I. Moved. On." Her chin was up. Her shoulders back. "I let his ghost go. Maybe it's time you learned to do the same." Then her phone rang, vibrating in her pocket. She turned away, yanking it from her pocket.

"Logan?" A brief pause, then, "Yes, we had to seek shelter in a shack on the south ridge."

Gunner ran a rough hand over his face. That had been too close for him. Far too close. Another few seconds, and he wouldn't have been able to pull away from her.

Another few seconds, and he wouldn't have cared about the secrets that hid in his heart or the guilt that ate him late at night.

Another few seconds, and he'd have taken her.

But he'd held strong. He could keep his control. He'd protect her, always watch out for her, just as he'd sworn to do.

Anything else wasn't possible. Even if he had to keep being the bastard who held Sydney at arm's length.

*Sometimes you can't have the one thing that you want most.*

Because you knew, deep down, that you didn't deserve that one thing.

SUNLIGHT STREAMED THROUGH the blinds, faint streaks of light that shot across the bed, and slid over Jasper's body.

And the body of the soft woman in his arms.

He didn't move when he first woke, too content to keep holding Veronica. He couldn't remember the last time he'd just held someone. Maybe because there wasn't a memory.

She was different.

And he was lying to her.

Hell.

The truth would come out, sooner or later. The truth would *always* come out. When he brought down her brother and the EOD agents took Cale away, what would he say to Veronica then?

*Sorry about Cale. Sorry about lying to you. But, hey, maybe we can still hook up? The sex was incredible.*

It was more than just the sex. More than just pleasure that he'd lose if he lost her.

*She's more than I thought.* She'd slipped under his guard. Strange, when he should have been the one guarding her.

"Why do you look sad?"

His body tensed. He hadn't even realized that she'd been awake. But his gaze rose to her face and he found her stare on him, seeing *into* him as few others had done.

"I'm worried about you." That was true, even if there was more involved. Worried about her safety, worried about losing her.

"Why? You're here to keep me safe, right? The big, bad ranger."

She made him smile. He bent and pressed a kiss to her cheek. "You're right—that's why I'm here." His smile faded. *To keep you safe and to bring down your brother.* Jasper cleared his throat. "We should head back to the main house. See if Wyatt has any more information for us."

She nodded and slowly pulled away from him. She sat up on the side of the bed, giving him a perfect view of her back and its elegant curve. "I don't regret anything that happened," she told him, and looked over her shoulder. "Just in case you were curious."

He rose slowly. The sheets bunched around his waist. "Remember that." His knuckles slid down her spine. Her skin was so smooth. She sucked in a little gasp when he pressed a kiss to the base of her back.

*Never another like her.*

He lifted his head. Rolled away to his side of the bed, then stood. "We'll head back to the house, check in with Wyatt, then start searching the rest of the property." Though he was curious about the progress that Sydney and Gunner might have made. They probably had been caught in the storm, too. But the team would be back in action soon.

He grabbed his jeans, jerked them on and yanked his shirt over his head. He heard the rustle of Veronica dressing behind him, and he just had to turn and enjoy the view.

*A virgin.* That news still shocked the hell out of him, but it also…made him happy. No one else had ever seen her eyes go blind with pleasure. No one else had heard her sweet gasps when her climax hit.

"What is it?"

She'd caught him staring at her.

Clearing his throat, Jasper told her the truth. He figured she deserved a truth from him. "You're beautiful." *And dangerous to me. So very dangerous.*

A flush of heat filled her cheeks, and then a warm smile spread over her lips. "You're pretty gorgeous yourself."

Right. The woman had seen all his scars. Kissed them. He still couldn't believe that she'd done that. She hadn't been repulsed or scared. She'd just been…loving.

Perfect.

He was so messing everything up with her. He knew it. His breath rushed out. He had to talk with Logan. Get permission from the EOD powers-that-be, aka Bruce Mercer—the bigwig Mystery Man who seemed to run Elite Ops—to brief Veronica fully on the situation with Cale.

She deserved the truth.

He couldn't, *wouldn't* keep lying to her.

Veronica was dressed now and staring at him a bit uncertainly as her smile wavered.

He walked toward her with slow, sure steps. She tilted her head back to look up at him. "You aren't what I expected," he told her.

"Is that good? Or bad?"

Both.

"Don't hate me, okay?"

Her brows rose. "Ah, is this typical morning-after etiquette for you? You tell a woman not to hate you because—"

"There's nothing typical about you." That was a big part of the problem. If she hadn't been getting under his skin, he could have kept playing his part, and he could have stayed the hell away from her last night.

But he'd wanted her too much.

A reckoning would come soon. He'd pay for that desire.

As soon as he got her to the main house, he was calling Logan and Mercer. No more secrets. No more lies.

Jasper pulled his gun and headed toward the door. He peeked through the blinds of the nearby window, searching the area outside. Then he moved to the other windows, scanning and checking.

"Do you think someone was watching us l-last night?" she asked him, voice suddenly hushed.

Giving a quick shake of his head, Jasper told her, "No, the storm was too bad. No one was out there." And it looked as though no one was out there now. He went back to Veronica, took her hand and led her outside.

The ground was still wet, heavy with mud, while standing water covered much of the area. Driving back to the main house would be tricky, but the truck would handle it. He cast a quick, worried glance at

Veronica. He didn't want her to have any bad memories if the truck started to slide.

She climbed into the truck, buckled her seat belt and said, "I'm fine, Jasper," in a determined way that told him she knew exactly what he'd been thinking.

He hurried around to the driver's seat. He secured his weapon and cranked up the vehicle. When the engine growled to life, he gently pushed down the gas even as he swept the steering wheel around in a large circle. The driving would be slow going—so damn slow—but he wouldn't take any risks with Veronica.

His gaze swept the area up ahead. The storm had knocked over trees, sent the stream to swelling and had pretty much ravaged everything in sight.

"It's funny," Veronica murmured. "Once we got together, I forgot all about the storm."

He started to smile.

But then he saw a glint up ahead. A flash of the sun on metal, one big white line that shouldn't be there. Swearing, he jerked the steering wheel to the right, but he made his move too late.

Gunfire exploded, and a bullet ripped through the windshield. Veronica screamed as the truck careened, rushing forward. The bullet had hit him, his blood was seeping out and he couldn't control the truck.

Couldn't stop it.

The truck slammed into a tree. Glass shattered and Veronica stopped screaming.

# Chapter Eight

She was trapped in the car.

*Mommy wasn't moving. Why wasn't she moving? Daddy?*

The nightmare of her past tangled with her present. Veronica's hands were against the dashboard. Broken glass was all around her.

*Mommy had been bleeding. She'd been so still.*

The seat belt bit into her shoulder.

*She couldn't get out of her seat. She was strapped in and she screamed and screamed because something was wrong. She couldn't get out.*

Her fingers fumbled. There was a click, and then the seat belt slid free. Her body sagged forward. The truck was at some kind of angle—it had slid down a little ravine and slammed into a tree.

Her forehead was wet. Her fingers lifted. Blood?

*Daddy had been bleeding.*

Her fingers fisted. She shoved the memory back into her mind. She wasn't a child anymore. And she wasn't alone.

Her head whipped to the right. "Jasper?" He was slumped over the steering wheel, not moving.

Had he been hurt in the crash or...*no, before the crash.* The memory of those desperate moments flooded through her. That sound that she'd heard hadn't been thunder. It had been a gunshot. One that had blasted through the windshield—and hit Jasper.

Carefully now, so very carefully, she pushed him back. The sunlight spilled through the broken windows so that she could clearly see his blood-soaked chest. "Jasper!" This time, her cry was desperate.

His lashes fluttered. "Ver...onica? What...happened?"

"Someone shot us." *You.* She tried to find his wound, but there was so much blood. She needed to put pressure on the wound. She had to stop the blood. That was what people always did on TV shows. Apply pressure. Stop the bleeding.

His eyes looked bleary. "Get...out..."

She leaned toward him. She was so scared that her whole body shook. "What? What is it?" There was a huge gash near the right side of his forehead.

"Have to...get out...shooter...coming..."

Her heart stopped.

"Disabled...vehicle...sitting duck..."

She didn't want to be a sitting duck, but Jasper had to be suffering from some kind of head trauma if he thought she was just going to run off and leave him there alone. Because then *he'd* be the sitting duck.

Her gaze flew around the truck's interior. Where was his cell phone? Hers? She fumbled next to his seat, found what she thought was his phone and— *smashed*.

His eyes began to sag closed again. *"Go..."*

The hell she was just going to leave him. They'd both go. She'd drag him out if she had to.

*And I think I have to.*

Veronica turned away from him and shoved against her door. It wasn't budging. She shoved again and again, and then she angled her body and kicked.

The door finally groaned open.

"Hold on," she told Jasper as she turned back to touch his cheek once more. Her fingers were covered with his blood. "I'm coming around to get you. We'll both get out of here." Somehow.

If she could just find her phone, maybe it would work and she could get Wyatt out there. He could help them.

She eased from the truck, glanced to the left, then the right. She didn't see anyone, but then, she hadn't seen the shooter, either. The blast had just exploded in the truck, wrecking her world.

*Daddy...Daddy!*

The memories just wouldn't stay buried. Her fingers curled over the door and she started to slide around the vehicle. The truck had crashed down in the small ravine, which definitely wasn't an advantage. A shooter could come up from higher ground and easily take them both out.

Jasper had been right. They were sitting ducks.

She eased toward the back of the truck. She bent low, trying to stay as covered as she could and—

Hard arms wrapped around her. Veronica opened her mouth to scream as she was yanked back against a strong chest. Her scream never escaped. A hand was pushed over her mouth, and the scream emerged as just a whimper of sound that was stifled beneath rough fingers. She kicked back with her legs and twisted frantically as she tried to escape that steely grip.

"Shhh…Ronnie, it's me."

The familiar voice froze her.

And terrified her.

Because it was her brother's voice.

"We have to get out of here," Cale said. His mouth was close to her ear. "The shooter's close, and I can't risk him taking a shot at you." His hold eased on her. His hand slipped away from her mouth. "Come on." His voice was the quietest of whispers. "We'll circle back and stay low behind the brush near the—"

"I'm not leaving Jasper." Her own voice was hushed, and she could barely hear it over the frantic beating of her heart. She wanted to grab Cale, to hold him tight, but she had to take care of Jasper. He needed her. "He's hurt, Cale," she said as she turned to face her brother. "We have to get him out of that truck, get him to safety—"

*"Step the hell...away from her."* Jasper's voice. Coming from right behind her.

She whirled and found him standing near the back of the vehicle, his face pale, his bloody shirt clinging to his chest.

He was also holding a gun. A gun that he had aimed right at her brother.

Veronica stepped into that line of fire. "Jasper, what are you doing? Cale is here to help us." She refused to acknowledge the fleeting terror she'd felt when she first heard his voice.

"Did you think the shot...took me out? That it was...safe to come and...get Veronica?" Jasper rasped.

The gun was aimed at Veronica now.

"Lower that weapon," Cale snarled.

Jasper lifted his left hand. Held his palm out to her. "Come here, Veronica."

If she moved, he'd have a clear shot at Cale. Cale was the only family she had. "Cale didn't do this," she said. "Jasper, you're hurt. Give me the gun and let us help you. Cale can give us cover—we can all get out of here alive."

Jasper shook his head. His eyes weren't on her. His gaze was focused over her shoulder. On Cale. "I don't...think...the plan is for us all to get out."

Cale swore behind her. His hands rose to her shoulders. He was trying to move her to the side. To get her out of Jasper's range.

She wasn't going easily.

Cale's grip tightened on her. "You've got a head wound, man. You don't know that you can take a clear shot." Cale's voice was ice-cold, but she still heard the hot fury undermining the words. He always became colder when he was angry. *"You could hit her."*

A muscle jerked in Jasper's jaw.

Then they all heard it…the growling of an engine, coming closer. Wyatt? Coming to help them? Or the shooter, coming to finish them?

She glanced back at Cale. He didn't have a weapon in his hands. Jasper was the only one with the gun, and he was pointing the weapon at the wrong people.

Veronica looked at Jasper once more. "Y-you were supposed to help me find Cale," she said, trying to get through to him. "Why are y-you doing this?"

"Because he's not here to find me." The instant response burst from Cale. "The EOD sent him to capture me."

The EOD? She didn't even know what that was, but—but the growling of that car's engine was growing louder.

Company was coming.

"That could be the shooter," she whispered as she stepped toward Jasper. Instantly, Cale's hands clamped down on her shoulders like a vise. She tried to shake him off. Not happening.

"Get. Away. From. Her," Jasper gritted.

"You're not going to shoot." Cale was confident. "You'd hurt her. You've never hurt a civilian in your life."

Was that all she was to Jasper? A civilian?

"I'll be back," Cale whispered in Veronica's ear. "Don't worry, I won't leave you on your own." Then he was pulling away, turning, running back for the brush that would give him cover until he reached the stream.

And Jasper was trying to follow him. No, Jasper was raising his weapon to shoot him.

"Stop!" she screamed. She leaped forward and placed her body directly in front of the gun. "Don't do it."

Jasper wrapped his hand around her wrist and jerked her to his side. She turned her head, desperate to see Cale.

But her brother hadn't made it to the brush. The woman with short blond hair—the woman Veronica had seen with the tech team at Last Chance—had just burst from that covering. She had her weapon up and dead-aimed on Cale. The federal agent, Gunner, was right by her side.

They'd stopped her brother. And they were...cuffing him?

"Jasper?" He'd finally lowered his weapon. He

stared at her with a carefully shielded gaze, one that she couldn't read no matter how hard she tried.

"I'm sorry," he told her.

"Don't be sorry! Tell me what's happening!" If he weren't wounded, she'd be shaking him.

The woman ran toward them. "Hell, Jasper, that looks bad." She had her phone out and was calling for backup and an EMT right away. Her gaze swept to Veronica. "You hurt?"

Yes. It felt as if someone were clawing out her heart. "Why is Cale in cuffs? He didn't shoot at us." She waved her hand in the air, pointing up toward the ridge. "You need to check up there for the shooter. We're all in danger out here. We've got to stop him and—"

"We checked the ridge. Right after we heard the crash. No one's there." The woman moved closer to Jasper. *Is she an agent, too?* "Figured you'd get shot. You always have to prove that you can take a bullet, don't you?"

"Bullet...in and out of my shoulder...it's my head that feels like it's...tearing apart."

Because his head had slammed into the steering wheel or the windshield. Veronica wasn't sure which. She wanted to comfort him, but the other woman was checking his wounds and Veronica wasn't sure what was happening. *Jasper pulled a gun on Cale.* Her gaze snapped toward her brother. Gunner was leading him away.

She was standing there, lost, and the full knowledge of what had happened slowly sank in for her.

The way the woman was talking to Jasper...

The reference Cale had made to the EOD...

The presence of the agents and their readiness to arrest Cale.

Her body trembled. Nausea rolled in her belly.

From the beginning, it had been a setup. Jasper had been hunting Cale, but not because he wanted to help her find her brother.

But because he wanted to arrest him.

"What's the charge?" Veronica whispered.

Jasper glanced over at her. His eyes glinted. "Veronica..."

"Multiple counts of murder," the blonde woman said, voice flat. "I'm sorry, Ms. Lane, but your brother is a killer, and we're taking him in."

That was the moment when her world came crashing down around her.

A LOCAL DOC, a lady with bright red hair, glowering eyes and tough hands, stitched Jasper up. It was the same doc who'd taken care of the kid who'd tried to abduct Veronica. Jasper railed the whole time she patched him up. He could feel a sledgehammer hitting his brain, but he didn't care about that pain or the burn of the bullet wound and stitches.

He wanted to get to Veronica.

He had to explain to her.

Back at the accident scene, she'd stared at him as if he were a stranger. Hell, to her, he was. A stranger that she'd taken to her bed, only to discover that he'd been lying to her all along. Using her.

*I'm so damn sorry, Veronica.*

Once the doc was through with him, Jasper headed over to meet up with the rest of his team. Even before the sheriff's station had been reduced to ashes and a few skeleton walls, the EOD agents had already scouted the area for their own headquarters. Now the EOD was set up in an old building, one that would serve as their base until the mission was over. When he entered their temporary headquarters, Jasper saw Logan sitting behind a desk in the main room. Sydney paced near him.

"That was close," Logan said, glancing at the bandage on Jasper's forehead and the covered wound on his shoulder. "I'm starting to wonder who has the bigger death wish, you or Gunner."

Jasper's jaw clenched. "Where's Veronica?"

"That's your question?" Logan's blue gaze narrowed. "We brought in our suspect. We even held off interrogation until *you* dragged your sorry hide out of the doc's office, and the first thing you ask about is the girl?" He gave a soundless whistle. "Interesting."

Jasper thought about punching Logan. Sure, Logan was their leader, the guy with the code name of Alpha One, but leader or not, he was still close to getting hit.

Logan rose from his chair and slowly came around the desk. "You didn't get emotionally involved in this one, did you?"

*Hell, yes.*

"Because we both know just how dangerous that can be," Logan said, memories flashing in his own eyes.

But in Logan's case, that emotional involvement had turned out okay. Logan had saved his lady, and they were planning to get married. Logan was on his way to that picket-fence dream.

Lucky bastard.

While Jasper was pretty sure any dreams he'd been dumb enough to have were dead.

"He asked for you," Sydney said.

Jasper glanced her way. Her gaze darted between him and Logan. "During his transport here," Sydney clarified, "the prisoner kept saying that he only wanted to talk with Jasper."

Well, that would explain why Logan hadn't started the interrogation. "Planning to use me, huh?" Jasper asked. But wasn't that the way the EOD worked? Before Logan could answer, Jasper focused on Sydney once more. "What about Veronica?" They'd been separated at the crime scene. Logan had insisted that Jasper go with the doctor—as if he hadn't spent plenty of time walking around with much worse wounds—while Veronica had stayed with the EOD agents.

"What about her?" Sydney asked, lifting her brows.

The woman was going to make him spell it out. She always enjoyed making him suffer a bit. Part of Sydney's charm. Or not. "Did she ask about me?" he gritted.

A hint of sympathy lit her gaze. "She asked if you were EOD."

Hell, hell, *hell.* "And you told her?"

"It's not my place to break that woman's heart more than it's already been broken." She stared directly at him. "That's your job." There was more heat in her voice than he usually heard.

Even Logan glanced at her with a touch of surprise.

"You know, it's not impossible to do a job without hurting a woman. You didn't have to sleep with her." Sydney's hands were fisted on her hips now. Yes, the woman was definitely angry. Odd, especially for controlled Sydney.

"She *told* you that?" he asked her.

"No, I could see it on her face." Sydney exhaled in a rush. "There's a certain kind of look that a woman gets when a lover betrays her. Your Veronica had that look."

"I need to talk to her." *Now.* He had to explain—

Logan shook his head. "We've got a plane coming

in at 0600 tomorrow. The EOD wants Cale brought in to the D.C. office for questioning and containment. That means we have less than twenty-four hours—" his eyes narrowed on Jasper "—to break the suspect."

Logan wanted him to do the breaking. That message was loud and clear in Alpha One's gaze.

"The first EOD agent that Cale killed…Marcus Holloway…he was a friend of mine." Logan's lips tightened. "We're not letting another team take this guy away. We're getting Cale's confession. *We're* closing this case."

Logan had always been territorial. When it came to the cases and his life.

Jasper had never really felt territorial about anyone or anything, until Veronica.

"We have everything here that we need to break him." Logan nodded at Jasper. "We've got you, Wyatt—the sheriff seems to be the guy's only friend—and we've got Cale's sister."

Jasper stiffened. "I'll talk to Cale." For all the good it would do. The man wasn't the breaking type. Most army rangers weren't. "But we aren't using Veronica."

Logan just stared back at him.

Angry, Jasper snarled, "Would you use Juliana?"

He saw the hit in Logan's eyes.

*That was what I thought.* "Veronica stays out of

this." He pulled in another breath, trying to slow his racing heart. "I'll handle Cale."

Then, because he didn't want to waste any more time on an already ticking clock, he glanced at Sydney. She pointed toward the narrow hallway. "Last door on the right. Gunner has guard duty."

He nodded, and squaring his shoulders, he headed down that hallway. Logan followed him, shadowing his steps. Jasper knew that Logan would want to hear every word of this interrogation. And, knowing Sydney, the room housing Cale had already been set up for full video and audio surveillance.

Everything that happened in that room would be recorded. Monitored constantly until Cale was on the flight heading to D.C.

Gunner opened the door for Jasper. Jasper and Logan stalked inside. A small table sat in the middle of the room. Cale was seated at the table, with his hands cuffed behind his back.

The room's windows had been boarded up. The only way in was through the door. The door that an armed Gunner was blocking.

Jasper pulled out a table chair, one directly across from Cale. No point in delaying. He sat down and met the glaring blue gaze of his prisoner.

Veronica's gaze was a bright sky-blue. Her brother...well, his blue gaze was dark and hard. Promising retribution.

"You used her," Cale said, body tense.

Jasper didn't speak. Just having Cale talk first was a victory in interrogation. When suspects wanted to talk, you let them. They usually talked too much, revealed too much.

And you just got to sit back and listen.

He'd learned all about interrogations during his two years at the EOD.

"You know how important Veronica is to me," Cale continued, his voice flat, totally emotionless, "and you knew she was always off-limits. She wasn't part of our world."

The world of battles and death. Blood and bullets.

Jasper leaned forward and felt the pull of his stitches. "You made her a part of that world when you started hunting EOD agents. You brought us right to her door." Or they would have gone to her door...

*But she came looking for me in that bar. Walked up to me with fear and determination mixed in her gaze, and she asked for my help.*

"You've got the wrong man." Cale gave him a smile that a tiger would have envied as he leaned back in his chair. "I haven't killed *any* EOD agents."

"That's not what the evidence says." Jasper kept his voice just as flat as Cale's. He wasn't giving the guy the upper hand.

Logan watched in silence from his position against the right wall. His arms were crossed over his chest, and his gaze was locked on Cale.

But Cale shook his head and seemed to ignore Logan. A trick, of course, because Jasper knew that Cale was aware of every move that the other agent made. Still staring right at Jasper, Cale said, "Evidence can lie. Especially if it's planted evidence."

"So someone's setting you up?" Jasper let the doubt drip from his words.

"If you weren't so busy screwing my sister, you would have realized that sooner."

Jasper hadn't expected the knife stab to come so fast. He took the jab and tilted his head to better study Cale. "You've been watching us."

Cale's eyes darkened with fury. *He didn't know. Hell. He was just guessing. Just tossing out—*

Cale leaped to his feet and slammed his head into Jasper's. Jasper punched him back, but not before Cale managed to connect hard with the fresh wound on Jasper's forehead.

Cale had never minded playing dirty.

Logan rushed forward and shoved Cale back into his seat. Then he took out his gun and aimed it right at Cale. "Go at my agent again, and you'll be a dead man. We won't care about hearing your side of the story. We won't care about—"

Cale's laughter cut through his words.

Jasper swiped away the blood that had dripped down from his forehead.

"You think I don't know this scene?" Cale asked, still grinning. "If you're questioning me, then you want something. Something you think only I can give you."

True enough. So why play any more games? "We want to know who hired you to kill the agents."

Cale's grin was chilling.

"You're a mercenary, right?" Logan pushed. "You kill for the right cash."

Cale's gaze slowly slid from Logan to Jasper. "I figure every man in this room has plenty of blood on his hands."

Jasper looked down at his hands. He'd washed blood away less than an hour before. Still looking at his hands, he said, "You were paid to kill three EOD agents. Marcus Holloway." He glanced up, waiting for a reaction. "Julian Forrest and Ben King."

Cale gave no reaction. "I didn't kill them."

"You knew them all," Jasper said. "That's why it was so easy to get close to them. Hell, what did they do? Just open their doors when they saw you? Told you to come on in? Then you attacked when they turned their backs?"

"That's not the way I attack."

"We found shoe impressions that you left at a scene. Clay that matched up to the exact same kind that you've got on your ranch." He heaved out a breath. "I guess you didn't clean up after yourself well enough at those scenes."

Cale stared back at him. "I don't kill men on my side."

"But they weren't on your side." This came from Logan. "They were on the EOD's side, and the EOD didn't want you."

Cale glanced over at him. "Is that the best you've got?"

"'Unstable,'" Jasper quoted, trying to divide Cale's attention. "'Extreme aggressive tendencies...'"

The tiger's smile flashed again. "Show me one ranger who isn't aggressive."

"Most rangers aren't put on warning lists by their shrinks."

"Yeah, well, most shrinks aren't looking for a little payback because you caught 'em messing around with an underage girl." One dark brow rose. "I had to let loose a few of my 'aggressive tendencies' that day."

What? Jasper kept his expression blank as surprise rolled through him. There hadn't been a record of any charge against the shrink. Had the guy really been involved with an underage girl? Or was Cale just trying to B.S. them?

"Check the story if you don't believe me." Cale was way too confident. "Dr. Paul Lyland lost his license a few months back. Seems someone got evidence on him, and the not-so-good doctor had to go before the review board. Pity his nose never healed properly," Cale muttered, as if the words were an afterthought. "But maybe that will serve as a reminder for the shrink. A reminder that plenty of folks are watching him now."

Watching and waiting for their pound of flesh? "Do you like delivering your own justice?" Jasper asked Cale, trying to figure him out.

Cale shrugged. "Somebody has to deliver it."

"Why not let that somebody be you?" They'd check the story on the shrink, but Jasper's instincts were telling him it was true. Hell, what else had they missed?

"Did those agents do something wrong, too?" Jasper asked because it had to be asked. "If we go digging in their pasts, are we gonna see that they did something to make them land on your punishment list?"

"I don't have a list."

"Don't you?" Jasper threw right back.

Cale's stillness seemed to be his only answer, but, after a tense moment, Cale said, "Guess who just got added?"

*Me.*

Cale leaned forward. "Now, I've played nice. And if you want me to keep playing nice, you'll bring my sister to me."

"I don't think so," Logan began.

Cale surged to his feet, seeming to completely ignore the gun that was inches from his face. "If I don't see Veronica, then I don't say another word. I know how this game works. Hell, you two think you can get to me? After the nightmare I survived in Syria? Think again."

Jasper pushed back his chair and slowly stood. "We'll see if Veronica wants to talk to you." He turned his back on Cale, a deliberate risk.

"If?" Cale snarled.

Jasper glanced over his shoulder, keeping his expression blank. He was as good at wearing an unfeeling mask as Cale was. *Maybe I'm better.* "Now that she knows just what you really are, do you still think she's gonna be the adoring little sister? Maybe it's time *you* think again."

He marched past Gunner, rage burning in his veins, the fire simmering just beneath his controlled exterior. Cale had once been his closest friend, but he sat across from him as an enemy.

And Veronica? What was she? Not an adoring little sister to Cale, and to him—

He rounded the corner and came face-to-face with her. She stood in the middle of the hallway, with Wyatt right by her. Sydney waited close by them.

Veronica gazed into Jasper's eyes, and her expression was cold. She'd never been cold before. She'd burned red-hot for him.

Now she seemed to look right through him.

## Chapter Nine

*Stay in control. Don't let him see your anger. Don't let him see your hurt.*

Veronica kept her chin up and her back ramrod straight. Wyatt had told her that the agents needed her at their headquarters. The EOD "headquarters" had turned out to be the abandoned building at the end of Black Bear Road.

Jasper was staring at her with blazing eyes. The female agent—the woman had finally introduced herself as Sydney Sloan—had sympathy on her pretty face as she edged closer. It was all Veronica could do not to start screaming at them.

But she was trying to follow another one of Cale's rules. *Never break in front of the enemy. Never show your pain. Others will just use that pain against you.*

Jasper had sure caused her plenty of pain.

"They're not FBI, you know that, right?" Veronica said to Wyatt. He'd been with her, pretty much from the moment since the agents had taken her brother into custody. At the crash scene, he'd appeared with

Logan Quinn. Wyatt's face had looked grim, the faint lines around his face much deeper.

"Not FBI," Wyatt agreed quietly, "but they've got high clearance."

"How high?" Veronica asked. She wasn't staring Jasper in the eye. She couldn't. And he was just staring at her.

"High enough that the governor called and told me to do whatever Logan Quinn said."

When the governor said jump...

She swallowed the lump in her throat. She'd been a fool, and now she had to pay a price for her blind trust.

*Talk to Jasper.* Because he was still just staring at her, waiting. "You're not a mercenary," she said, and risked the briefest of stares into his eyes.

"No, ma'am."

She flinched at that drawl. Her gaze dropped to his chin.

His jaw clenched.

"What are you?" she asked him.

"I'm a federal agent."

"You're *not* with the FBI."

"No, ma'am."

Her eyes slit as they lifted back to meet his gaze. "What's the EOD?"

He glanced at the sheriff. Yes, she knew that Wyatt could tell her, especially since it seemed that he, Logan and the governor were all suddenly tight, but she wanted to hear this information straight from Jasper. It would be interesting to see what the truth sounded like from him.

"It's the Elite Operations Division. We're a hybrid group, mostly ex-military."

Like her brother. "Why were you hunting Cale?"

He reached for her. She flinched back. He was bleeding. There was blood on his forehead, and she'd noticed that his shoulder looked padded—probably because of a bandage under his shirt.

His hand dropped.

"Why?" she repeated.

"Because Cale is wanted in connection with the murders of three EOD agents."

She shook her head instantly. "He wouldn't do that," she whispered, but she cleared her throat and spoke again, her voice stronger. "Cale rescues people. He doesn't kill them. He doesn't—"

"We also think he's tied to the fire and explosion at the police station, and the murder of the two men who were shot outside the station—the men who attempted to abduct you." A clipped voice.

She wanted to rage at him, but her voice stayed controlled. Mostly. "*I* was outside that station. Do you seriously think my brother was trying to kill me, too?"

"No, ma'am."

Veronica *hated* that drawling "ma'am" bit.

"I think your brother is one fine shot," Jasper

continued quietly. "Actually, I *know* he is. That's why you weren't hurt that day. He took out his targets, just like this morning, when he aimed only at me, not you."

Her cheeks felt icy. "I was inside the station when the fire started, the explosion—"

"Your brother had demolitions training when he was in the military."

She didn't want to hear this.

"He would have known how to stage that scene. Sydney talked to an arson investigator. The initial flames were set to alert folks in the station. To give us time to get out. But the explosion that followed, that was designed for a specific type of destruction. A bomb was placed, then triggered so that the back of the station would be hit hardest. The bomber knew exactly what he was doing. Hell, we even think the guy used a cell phone to start the explosion in the back."

The back of the station. She'd been in the front, so...

"Your brother made sure you were clear in that explosion. He protected you, but still went after the men he wanted."

This couldn't be true. "I want to see him." Because Jasper was *wrong*.

"Good, because he wants to see you, too."

Her heartbeat wouldn't slow down. It was racing too hard in her chest, and her hands were trembling.

Jasper motioned toward the far end of the hallway. "Come this way."

Fine. She stepped forward. Instantly, Wyatt moved with her. He'd been silent during the exchange with Jasper. Watching, weighing every word. Did everyone but her think that Cale was a monster? A cold-blooded killer?

Soldier...or sociopath.

Jasper slammed his hand into the sheriff's chest. "Sorry, Wyatt, for now, it's just her."

Wyatt frowned at him. "That's my friend in there. If he's gone rogue, I can get him to talk."

*He hasn't gone rogue.*

But Jasper shook his head. "For now, I'm only taking Veronica back to interrogation."

Wyatt's gaze cut to Veronica. Frustration etched hard lines on his face. "You going to be okay in there?"

She nodded. She wasn't about to break apart. Yes, Jasper's betrayal made it feel as if he had tried to carve out her heart, but she *wouldn't* break. Jasper wrapped his hand around her elbow and guided her down the hall. She didn't need his guidance. She didn't need anything from him anymore.

"In here." He pushed open a door to the left. She entered, rushing in her eagerness to see Cale, only... Cale wasn't there. The room was empty.

She spun around just as Jasper shut the door behind him, sealing them inside.

"We need to talk," he said.

Her hands were fisted so hard that her knuckles hurt. "I want to see my brother. You told me—"

"You will see him." The words were rough. "But first, you're going to talk to me."

He started to close in on her. Instinctively, Veronica backed up a step, but then she froze. He wasn't going to intimidate her, not anymore. "You should wipe that blood away," she muttered, her gaze rising to his forehead. "It really messes up that whole intense, scary vibe that you're trying to give me."

He stopped and frowned at her.

And she was lying. The blood just made him look more dangerous and scary. But so what if she was lying? He'd lied; she could do it, too. Maybe it was childish, but she didn't care.

"The blood's a little gift from your brother," Jasper murmured. "Seems he doesn't like the fact that we're involved."

Her brows shot up. "We're not." What had he told her brother? Oh, no, did Cale think that she'd been setting him up, too?

Jasper resumed his stalking moves toward her. "We most definitely *are*." The last word was bit out. "Or did you forget that you gave me your virginity just a few hours ago?"

He had *not* just said that to her.

"You waited," he continued, voice thickening, "because you wanted to be with the right man."

"You aren't the right man." She could barely force the words past her suddenly desert-dry throat. "What you are… You're a man who lied to me. From the first moment I saw you in that bar, everything has been a lie."

"Not everything." He was less than a foot away from her. Not touching. She didn't want him to touch her. It was hard enough to keep her wall of ice in place. She didn't want him touching her again and trying to shatter that wall.

"You're EOD." She threw that out at him.

He nodded.

"You think my brother is a killer."

"I know he is."

"Just like you are." Her breath heaved out. "He was following mission orders, saving lives. You said yourself that a soldier—"

"I'm not talking about lives taken during battle. I'm talking about murder. About going right up to a man and slitting his throat or stabbing him in the heart."

She remembered Reed Montgomery's body. The brutality. The blood. "Y-you're wrong."

"I want to be."

Her eyes met his in surprise. She held his stare. It was the first time she'd looked deeply into his eyes since realizing the truth.

Jasper shook his head. "I want to be wrong about Cale, but the evidence says I'm not."

"M-maybe the evidence is wrong." It had to be wrong.

"There's a lot of evidence, and every bit of it points to your brother."

Nails in his coffin. Or hers. She forced her hands to unclench. "Why were you sent in?"

"I belong to a special unit at the EOD, a unit some call the Shadow Agents. When the other EOD agents were murdered, the cases didn't go public. Our boss wanted us to handle this in-house. He wanted my team to find and apprehend the killer." Jasper's hand lifted, as if he'd touch her. But when she tensed, his hand fell back to his side. "When we realized exactly who we were after, it was decided that'd I'd be point on the mission because of my past relationship with Cale."

"And using me, that was just part of the plan, too, right?"

His green gaze glinted. "I knew Cale. I knew how he felt about you—"

"So you knew you could use me." She tried to walk around him. He grabbed her shoulders. Spun her back to face him.

The ice began to crack.

"I knew that your brother wasn't just going to cut and run and leave you behind." His fingers curled around her shoulders, pulling her closer. "I knew that he'd have to come back for you, sooner or later."

"So all you had to do was wait. Wait, and he'd be

here." *Sooner or later.* She swallowed to try to ease that dang dryness in her throat. "Why did you have to go so far?" Her voice came out too soft. "Why did you have to make love to me?"

"Because I wanted you, wanted you more than I wanted anything else."

She *wanted* to believe him.

"There's the mission." His head lowered toward her. "There's the job that I have to do and then there's you and me. There's what we feel."

He was going to kiss her. The ice was too weak around her. She couldn't handle this. Him.

Her hand slammed into his chest. "You lied to me."

His muscles were rock-hard beneath her hand.

*I was falling for you, and now I think everything was a lie.* "I don't get close to people easily. I—I can't." She'd always held back, was too shy, too cautious. "With you, everything seemed easy." She'd been too trusting. So ridiculously grateful to have someone finally on her side.

"It can be that way again," he growled. "Veronica…"

"Are you still working me?"

He frowned at her.

"Because I think you are. I think you and the other agents… I think you're about to take me in there to see my brother, and you're going to try and use me to get a confession from him."

She might be trusting, might be too naive, but she wasn't stupid.

And Jasper wasn't denying her charge.

"There's you and me," she said, pushing his words back at him, "and there's my brother. There's his case. It's all mixed together, and no matter what we might both want…" Because she did wish things were different. "They can't ever be separate."

Because touching him burned through her ice, she pulled her hand away from him. "Now, if you aren't taking me to see my brother, then I'll go find someone else who will."

He growled. No other word for it.

Fine. She started walking for the door.

"This isn't over," he warned.

Veronica didn't look back at him, but she did say, "You're right. It's not over. It won't be over until I prove my brother's innocence."

The floor creaked behind her. Then he was there, pulling open the door, leaning toward her. His lips brushed over the curve of her ear as he whispered, "I meant between us. You and I aren't close to being done."

The words were a threat. Swallowing, she lifted her chin and forced herself to walk slowly, calmly, down the hallway and toward her brother's holding room.

"I'M GUESSING THAT didn't go so well," Logan muttered as Jasper followed Veronica out of the room.

Logan offered Jasper a white cloth. "For the blood," Logan said, giving a nod of his head.

Jasper swiped the blood away.

"Focus on the case," Logan said. "Then go after the girl."

Because of the case, he was losing the girl. He tossed the cloth into the garbage and followed Veronica down the hallway. She'd stopped in front of Gunner. He was still guarding the door to Cale's room.

"Is he in there?" Veronica asked Gunner.

Jasper hated the flat tone of her voice. That wasn't Veronica. There was always emotion bubbling in her voice and eyes.

Not now.

Gunner glanced over at Jasper. He nodded. They had to do this. Logan wouldn't follow them in this time. He'd hang back, and Jasper knew he would be entering the surveillance room that Sydney had set up. The better to watch and see what was happening. The better to record any confessions that Cale might make.

Jasper saw Veronica suck in a deep breath right before Gunner opened the door and waved her inside.

*"Ronnie!"* Cale was instantly on his feet.

Veronica ran toward him with her arms open.

Jasper grabbed her, wrapping his arms around her waist and hauling her back. It was protocol, especially after Cale's attack on him. No touching. But when Veronica started twisting and fighting in his arms, she broke his heart.

*Since when do I have one of those?*

"Let her go!" Cale snarled. But he wasn't advancing on Jasper. Probably because an armed Gunner was blocking his path.

"I'll let her go," Jasper snarled right back, then bent to whisper in Veronica's ears, "I'll let you go." He cleared his throat, then said loud enough for everyone to hear, "But you can't touch him, Veronica. He's too dangerous."

"I'm not dangerous to my own sister!" Cale yelled.

She stopped fighting in Jasper's arms.

Slowly, carefully, Jasper released her.

Gunner put his hand on Cale's shoulder and forced him back into his seat. Jasper pulled out a chair for Veronica. She sat down and tucked her hands in her lap. She looked so vulnerable and sad, and he wanted to punch someone.

*Me.* Because he was the one who'd done this to her. She wasn't even looking at him the same way any longer. Before, her eyes had seemed to light up when she looked at him. He hadn't even noticed that light, not until it was gone.

*I want it back.*

He yanked a chair close to her. Made sure that his shoulder rubbed against hers. Cale's narrowed stare said he noted the move. His clenched jaw said it infuriated him.

"I missed you," Veronica told her brother, voice soft.

Cale's eyelids flickered.

"I—I was worried that something had happened." Her voice wasn't flat now. Emotion trembled beneath her words.

Cale gave her a smile, one that looked forced. "You know I'm hard to kill."

Yes, he was.

Her lips trembled.

Cale's face appeared to grow even harder. "Don't listen to anything that they tell you, Ronnie. I haven't killed any agents. You know me better than that."

She nodded.

"I didn't do it," Cale told her, eyes bright. "Tell me you believe me."

"I do." So soft. So true.

Her trust in her brother made Jasper furious and envious. So much unquestioning trust. She'd trusted him like that, too. For too short of a time. "She hasn't seen all the evidence that we have on you," Jasper said as he leaned back in his chair. Cale's body was tight and tense, so Jasper tried to appear just the opposite. Relaxed and unconcerned.

Relaxed was the last thing he felt.

"The evidence was planted." Cale's instant response. "You know I didn't—"

"Do you have any alibis that you'd like to give us? I mean, I know Logan was in here earlier and he told you the dates of all the murders. If you've got witnesses who can cover for you…"

Cale's gaze cut to his. "I don't have any alibis."

"Not the social sort, huh? Too bad. Some witnesses sure would have come in handy."

Veronica flinched beside him.

"But we actually already knew that you didn't have any alibis." Jasper shrugged. "Though we were waiting to hear some creative story."

Cale's stare returned to Veronica. "When I first left, I thought I was going out on a rescue mission."

Jasper didn't tense. This was what the team had hoped would happen. Cale didn't want Veronica to lose faith in him. So he'd tell her anything. Everything?

"I flew down to the Caribbean under the radar. I was supposed to be pulling out some businessman who was being held for a ransom that his family couldn't pay." His shoulders rolled as if he were pushing his way through the memory. "But when I got there, there was no businessman. No trail to indicate he'd ever been taken or that the guy even existed. It was a B.S. mission. One designed to get me out of the country." His head tilted toward Veronica. "And one to make sure I had no alibi. Because I was sent out just two days before the first murder."

"Nice story," Jasper murmured. He noticed that

no change of expression crossed Gunner's face. He wasn't buying the tale, either.

Of course, Veronica was buying every single word.

"Who sent you on the mission?" Veronica asked.

Cale hesitated.

Right. Because Jasper knew this part. "Let me guess, a dead man?"

Cale kept his gaze on Veronica. "Am I supposed to act surprised to hear that Reed Montgomery is dead?"

"Well, no," Jasper murmured. "Especially since you killed him and left his body for your sister to find, I don't see why you'd be—"

"I'm sorry, Ronnie." Cale's low voice, cutting right through Jasper's words. "You shouldn't have found him."

"Is that a confession?" Gunner asked at once, locking his stare on their suspect. "You killed him, but you didn't intend for Veronica to find the body?"

"No confession," Cale snapped. "I'm just sorry she was the one to see him like that." He shook his head and never took his eyes off Veronica. "I always tried to keep that part of my life away from you. I never wanted you to be hurt by it."

"I know," Veronica said. "You always protected me." A pause. "This time, I'll protect you." Her head turned and her gaze found Jasper's. "Why doesn't my brother have a lawyer? None of this is legal. You can't—"

Cale laughed. "This isn't on the books. This case will *never* be. They'll just toss me in a cage somewhere and let the world forget all about me."

Her face paled. "The hell they will. You aren't doing this to him. Cale is innocent!" She stood abruptly, sending her chair crashing to the floor. "I'm going to prove it."

Not what Jasper had hoped to hear. In fact, those words could put Veronica right in the middle of a very deadly mission.

CALE LANE HAD to die. There was no option. But then, Cale had been marked for death from the beginning. He just hadn't realized it.

He was in there with the EOD agents—cuffed, locked up, trapped.

Maybe he should just go in right now and kill him. He could say that Cale broke free...that the man came at him... The agents would probably buy his story.

But would Veronica? She was the problem.

Killing her hadn't been part of his plan. He'd wanted to keep her out of the game, but she was too protective of Cale. Too determined to find the "real" killer.

She didn't realize just how close the killer was to her. *Maybe it's time for me to get closer.*

He'd seen the way the agent, Jasper, looked at Veronica. The guy wanted her. Maybe Veronica could be used against him. She could sure be used against Cale; he already knew that.

The question was…just how did he want this game to end?

With Veronica alive or dead?

## Chapter Ten

Veronica frowned down at the computer screen, even as her heart beat in excitement. She'd pulled out the flash drive she'd taken from Reed Montgomery's place. Searched through all the files, and she'd found proof that her brother had been telling the truth about his mission to the Caribbean.

At least, she thought she might have proof. She'd found a notation for "Striker" heading to Jamaica the week her brother had vanished. The same week that Marcus Holloway had been killed. Jasper had told her that Holloway had been in Jamestown, Tennessee, when he was murdered, and, sure enough, she'd found a notation in the "Chances" file for a job in Tennessee that same week. Only instead of "Striker" being listed on that mission, Reed had typed in "Striker Two" as the code name. "Striker Two" was also the code name used for the mission to West Virginia and the mission to Phoenix.

Veronica thought that Reed had been differentiating between two separate mercenaries. Striker, her brother, and whoever Striker Two was. Because the Striker Two notations hadn't started to appear until the last six months. Someone else had been using that name, she was sure of it.

*Someone who was trying to frame my brother?* And had Reed been in on that framing? It looked as though he had.

She grabbed the phone. Started to call Jasper, then realized she didn't have the number for the EOD headquarters in town. So she called Wyatt instead. The sheriff would be with the agents. He could help her.

Wyatt's phone was answered on the second ring, only it wasn't Wyatt doing the answering. "Sheriff Halliday," a rough voice said, breaking up a bit.

She frowned. "Jimmy? Jimmy, is that you? This is Veronica Lane."

"It's me," he said at once, voice clearer, more alert. "Something wrong, Ms. Veronica?"

*Yes. Everything.* "I need to talk to the sheriff."

"He's back there with them agents talking to…" Jimmy cleared his throat. "He's talking to your brother. I think they're interrogating him." Dropping his voice, he said, "I heard 'em talking. They're gonna charge Cale with all them murders."

"Tell them to stop!" The words burst from her. "I've got proof—" *Maybe, please, let it be some proof.* "I've got proof to back up Cale's story about being in the Caribbean! Files I took off Reed Montgomery's computer. I just... I need to talk to Wyatt or Jasper. *Someone* there. I can prove Cale's innocence."

"You got real proof?" Jimmy's voice cracked with excitement.

"Yes." She wouldn't tell him that it wasn't one hundred percent. That it was just a few notations in a file, but...*it was something.* Bread crumbs that could lead them in the right direction. To the real killer. "I think Reed Montgomery was murdered because he could back up Cale's story about being out of the country. I think he knew the real killer's identity."

Lightning flashed, illuminating her living room. The storms weren't over. Another day, that was what the weather forecaster had promised. *Another day.*

"Is Jasper there?" Veronica asked. She could talk to him and—

"I don't know where he is, but, Ms. Veronica, I'll go get the sheriff. I'll tell him what you found. We'll clear Cale."

Jimmy had always seemed to look up to her brother. When he'd been younger, Jimmy had often come to the ranch, dogging Cale's footsteps, asking to hear stories about Cale's time in the army. Jimmy was a good guy, and he knew Cale for the real person that he was.

Yes, yes, they'd clear Cale. The nightmare would be over.

She hung up the phone and headed back for her

desk. She pulled the flash drive away from the computer and tucked it in her pocket. She could stay at her house and wait for Jasper or the sheriff, or she could go to them. Force them to see the proof that she had.

The lightning flashed again, and every light in her house went dark.

*I'm coming, Cale.* Fumbling, she found a pair of car keys. The keys were for the old sports car Cale kept covered in the garage. The car hadn't been used in over a year, but it was her only option at the moment. Cale and his cars...her brother had always been obsessed with them, and he'd made sure to share his expertise with her, too.

Then she rushed out of the house. The rain hadn't started, but the wind was already strong. She wouldn't think about the rough roads or the wind that could push the car too hard.

She'd just think of Cale. This time, she'd protect her brother.


CALE WAS GIVING them nothing. Figured. A ranger like him, Jasper knew exactly what sort of training the guy had been through over the years.

A few tough questions weren't going to rattle him. Not after he'd survived torture.

*Yeah, Cale, I still remember Syria.* Some things could never be forgotten.

Back then, Cale had been one of the good guys. What the hell had happened to him?

Jasper glanced back down the hallway toward Cale's holding room. Once, he never would have said that Cale would snap and start killing innocents.

"The story checked out," Sydney said as she walked out of the surveillance room. She had a fist-ful of papers. "Just got the fax on Dr. Paul Lyland. The guy did lose his license about eleven months ago."

Jasper ran a hand through his hair. "So the shrink's profile was bull?"

"No, I'd say Cale Lane has some definite aggressive tendencies." Her stare was knowing. "Just like you."

His back teeth clenched. "Dr. Lyland wasn't the only shrink who came up with this profile."

"No, but he was the most vocal, and if Cale had already been burned by one shrink, his hostile behavior to the others is more understandable."

Maybe.

"If he's telling the truth about this, then do you think he could be telling the truth about the case in the Caribbean?" Sydney asked him.

Jasper hesitated. The thing was…he *wanted* Cale to be telling the truth. He wanted Cale to be innocent. Because then Veronica wouldn't look so broken, and he wouldn't have been so dead wrong about a friend. "I'm going back in," he said. And because this needed to be off the record, he added, "Cut the surveillance, Sydney."

Her eyes widened. "Are you sure about that?"

He nodded. "This is personal."

"Hasn't it always been?" she murmured as he walked away.

VERONICA'S HANDS GRIPPED the steering wheel for dear life. The rain had started to fall again. Heavy, fat drops that hit her windshield faster than the wipers could clear the glass. The flash drive was in her pocket, and her body was strung so tightly that she felt she was about to jump out of her skin.

Only about ten more miles to go. Ten more, and then the main strip of the town would come into view.

She heard brakes squealing, an engine growling; then bright lights appeared on the dark road before her. Those lights looked as though they were coming right at Veronica. Panicking, she jerked the wheel to the right. The sports car bounced, slid off the shoulder of the road and the tires rolled in the thick mud.

The other driver—the car with the bright lights flashing—drove right past her. He didn't even slow to see if she was all right.

Her breath panted out. She'd braked. When had she braked? She took her foot off the pedal and cautiously touched the accelerator. The tires spun in the mud. She could hear the grinding sound, only…

She wasn't moving.

Veronica pushed down harder on the accelerator. More spinning, but the vehicle wasn't moving forward.

Her head rapped into the steering wheel. Just her luck. She'd gone out in the car, headed off the side of the road—

*And I didn't think about my parents.*

The breath stilled in her lungs. There'd been no flashback this time. She hadn't panicked. She'd gotten off the road, avoided the wreck.

A smile curved her lips even as a tear leaked past her eye. Maybe she was getting stronger. Finally.

Or maybe after the crash with Jasper, she just realized that the past wasn't what could hurt her. She had too much in the present to fear.

Exhaling heavily, she turned off the car, climbed outside. Ignoring the pounding from the rain, Veronica hurried around to the car's passenger side. One look, and she knew her car wouldn't be going any place soon.

The storms had washed away too much of the dry grass. Only mud remained, and her tires could spin for hours, but the car wasn't getting out of that mess without one very strong tow.

*Ten miles to go.*

So she'd better get to walking.

JASPER SLOWLY CLOSED the door behind him. He'd left his weapon outside and told Gunner to take a hike.

He wanted to be alone for this little chat.

Cale looked up at him and sighed. "Back to this, are we?" He rolled his shoulders. The handcuffs had been removed a few hours ago. A show of trust that Logan had hoped would get him talking. Cale had even been given two meals. Plenty to eat and drink.

The show of trust wasn't working. They were now down to less than ten hours before his transfer to D.C.

Jasper didn't bother sitting this time. He just stared at Cale. "I can still remember the scent of the jungle. The mix of rotting vegetation and blood."

Cale didn't speak.

"You were screaming at me, telling me that a bullet to the chest shouldn't slow down a real ranger, and you had a grip of steel on my arm."

Cale's expression had frozen.

"You could have left me to die there." Jasper shook his head. "All I did was slow you down, but you…you didn't give up on me."

"We were both too young and stupid to realize we should only be looking out for ourselves." Cale's voice was clipped.

"I don't think so." Jasper took a step toward him. "Veronica told me that you saved lives. That you went out, rescuing hostages." Work not too different from the EOD's. Only the EOD agents had the backup of the federal government. While Cale had been on his own.

*Easy pickings.*

"Is this where you do your good-agent routine?" Cale asked with a touch of curiosity. "Where you remind me that we were friends once so I should trust you?"

"We *were* friends."

Cale inclined his head. Jasper figured he'd take that as agreement. "Your story about the shrink checked out."

"You seem surprised," Cale murmured.

"Because you look good for these kills." He hesitated, then admitted, "Too good."

Cale's expression never altered.

"I've seen you on missions," Jasper said. "I know how you operate. You can walk for twenty miles, and never leave so much as a trace of your presence." And that had been nagging at him all along. But he'd stuck to the mission, followed orders.

Perhaps it was time he forgot the orders and focused on getting to the truth.

"You could do that so easily in the jungle, in the desert, in every damn place we went, but yet you left all this evidence behind at the murder scenes."

"Not *me*," Cale snapped. "The person who is setting me up. That's the guy who left all this so-called 'evidence' crap behind. Because he wanted to frame me."

"I *want* to believe you."

"Why?" Cale tossed back at him, eyes hard and challenging. "So my sister might forgive you? Because you think you might have a chance with her if you can exonerate me now…after you're the one who had me tossed in here?"

"You're staying in custody," Jasper said, just so they were clear. "And I'm staying on this case. Either I'll find enough evidence to guarantee your guilt, beyond any doubt—" any doubts that Jasper might have himself "—or I'll find the one who's framing you." He flattened his palms on the table. "But I'm going to need some help. You got enemies? Someone who could pull this off? Give me names."

Cale shook his head. "Veronica is too good for you."

He knew that.

"You'll break her heart. Head out on another mission and never look back."

He wanted to punch the wood, shatter the table. "This isn't about Veronica." *A lie.* If it weren't for her, would he even be having this conversation? "You say you're innocent, then help me. Give me a witness, give me *something.*"

"Reed Montgomery was my witness. He's the one who sent me to the Caribbean. He's the one who knows I wasn't in the country when the first agent was killed."

"Then why did his log have you in West Virginia

when Julian Forrest was killed? In Phoenix at the time of the hit on Ben King?" Because when he'd been back at Reed Montgomery's apartment, Jasper had looked over Veronica's shoulder and seen those clear notations. Striker Two…West Virginia. Striker Two…Phoenix. When Sydney got to digging into the machine, Jasper figured she'd find even more evidence.

Cale shook his head. "Not. Me."

"Then someone's sure doing a good job of pretending to be you." Maybe that was it. Damn it, maybe… Because Cale's code name was Striker. So why had Reed tacked on the "Two" handle? *Because someone else was taking those missions? Someone who could be just as deadly as Striker?* "Who is it? Who knows you well enough to trap you like this?"

Cale's lashes lowered. "You mean a man who knows how I kill? How I hunt? Who knows where to find evidence that can incriminate me, even as he leaves no evidence behind that would ever link *him* to the crimes?" Cale looked up at Jasper. "Well, old buddy, your name is the first one that springs to mind."

Hell.

"It's not—" Jasper began.

The door flew open. Jasper whirled around. Sydney stood in the doorway, her cheeks flushed, her breath heaving. "Jasper, I need you." Gunner was right behind her.

Casting one last, hard look at Cale, Jasper hurried from the room. Gunner slipped inside, resuming his guard duty.

"What is it?" Jasper asked her.

"We've got a problem." She marched down the hallway, passed the small lobby area, then headed upstairs. This was her workspace. He knew that Sydney always liked privacy when she worked with her computers and—

A whistle slipped from him when he saw the destruction. "What the hell happened?"

She headed toward the laptop—Reed Montgomery's laptop. The machine had been smashed, again and again, broken into sharp, hard pieces. Keyboard buttons were on the floor. It looked as if the machine's hard drive had been hit repeatedly with a hammer.

"Someone didn't want me seeing evidence," she said, putting her hands on her hips. "I don't know if it was luck or whoever did this knew just what he was doing, but he smashed the platters inside the hard drive." She looked back at Jasper. "It's highly unlikely that I'll be able to recover any information from this machine."

"When?" A snarl from him.

"I was up here less than two hours ago. Logan wanted that intel on the shrink, so I had to leave before I could start processing the computer."

Every muscle in his body was on high alert. "Only the EOD agents had access to this building."

"The agents…" She nodded, but said, "The sheriff. The deputy…and Veronica Lane."

He was already shaking his head. "It wasn't her."

"Maybe she was trying to help her brother, by hiding his guilt."

*"It wasn't her."* And there it was…blind trust. The same kind of trust Veronica had for Cale. The same kind of trust she'd given to Jasper just twenty-four hours ago. He spun for the door. "Where's the sheriff?"

"Gone." Her footsteps rushed after him. "Both Wyatt and the deputy went out to do some patrols. Logan is looking for them now but…"

He glanced back over his shoulder.

"I think you should be the one who brings Veronica in for questioning," Sydney said, eyes wide.

"It's not her." He knew it with every fiber of his being. But if it wasn't Veronica, and Cale couldn't have smashed the machine because he'd been in custody, then someone else out there was trying to make sure that Cale Lane wasn't cleared.

*"Someone is setting me up."* Yeah, Jasper was starting to believe Cale's words.

"As soon as Logan finds the sheriff and deputy, I want to know." He hurried down the stairs.

"Jasper! What about Veronica—"

"I'll take care of her." Sydney could interpret that any way she wanted.

Jasper grabbed his keys and raced out into the night.

VERONICA'S SHOULDERS HUNCHED as she walked. She was soaked through, and the wind and rain seemed to slap at her face with every step that she took.

She didn't have a cell phone. It hadn't been recovered after the crash at the ranch. And no one was on this road to help her.

People were too smart to be out in the storm.

The flash drive was still in her pocket. She'd been too afraid to leave it behind in the car. It was her only evidence. She *had* to hold on to it.

She heard the growl of a motor behind her. *Yes. Finally someone!* Veronica hurried back onto the road. The car was a good distance away now. She waved her arms as soon as the headlights hit her.

The headlights were so bright.

*As bright as they'd been before, when the car had come rushing at her.*

She froze, with her arms still over her head. The car wasn't slowing. The driver had to see her, even through the rain, but he wasn't slowing.

Veronica ran back toward the side of the road. Just as she left the pavement, she slipped in the mud and fell down hard. Mud soaked her clothes, and it felt as if her shoulder slammed into a rock, but she dragged herself forward to the row of trees near the edge of the road.

Behind her, brakes squealed as the car stopped. Her heartbeat echoed in her ears. Maybe the driver had seen her. Maybe he was coming to help her and she was panicking over nothing.

*Maybe.*

Cautiously, she turned back around. Because of the darkness, she could see very little about the car. The vehicle seemed low to the ground, with a long hood and a stretching trunk, but she couldn't determine the car's color or make. Veronica inched a bit closer. "Hello?" she called out. The driver's door had opened. She'd heard it creak.

And, over the rain and her racing heartbeat, she seemed to hear footsteps.

She pressed her muddy hands against her jeans. "Hello?" Veronica tried again.

But there was no response. She crept forward, just a little, and a sudden blast of gunfire ripped right past her head. Veronica slammed into the earth instantly.

Her breath heaved in her lungs. *He shot at me.* She remembered the eyes of the men who'd died before her.

Footsteps thudded toward her.

That was no Good Samaritan up there, coming to help a stranded motorist. Her instincts had been right about that.

Whoever it was out there…he was hunting her.

Carefully, she slid back into her cover. The line of trees was thin, and wouldn't provide her much protection. She glanced to the left, to the right. If she tried to run away from the road, she'd be running straight into the middle of nowhere. And the shooter could just follow her. Then what would she do?

*Die.*

Her gaze went back to the road even as she began to creep to the left, a path that would take her away from the shooter's car and—

Another shot blasted. Veronica stopped trying to creep away. He had a lock on her. Creeping wasn't going to work.

So she just ran. Dodging left and right, the way her brother had always told her she should run if someone was ever shooting at her.

Another Cale Lane rule…*"Never give 'em a steady target. The more you move, the harder it is for them to hit you."*

So she moved as fast as she could, dodging in between the trees, never moving in a straight line and praying, *praying,* that someone would come along soon to help her.

Then…then another vehicle's rumbling engine cut through the wind and rain.

When he heard the gunfire, Jasper's foot slammed down even harder on the accelerator. His windshield wipers sliced through the rain, and he kept a strong grip on the steering wheel. He hadn't been able to reach Veronica at her home. The phone had just rung and rung. Every ring had made him more afraid.

There was another roll of thunder—no, hell, another blast of gunfire. He knew that familiar sound too well. He rounded a curve, headed hard and fast down the long, narrow road. He didn't see anyone, not yet.

Then his lights cut across the darkness and the rain, and there was a shadow, a person, running right into the road. Running right at his vehicle.

He slammed on his brakes, and in that one frozen instant of time, Jasper was able to see her face.

*Veronica.* Terrified.

So afraid that she'd just run right into the path of a car. He jerked the wheel to the left, determined not to hit her, and his rental car bounced twice, then came to a jarring halt in the thick sludge of mud on the shoulder of the road.

Grabbing his gun, he leaped from the vehicle. *"Veronica!"*

Before his booted feet could even touch the asphalt, a car came racing right by him, sending him leaping back. The car's engine screamed and the smell of burnt rubber filled his nose. He had a fast impression of a black car, long and lean, slicing right through the night and rain.

*No tag.*

Then the car was gone. Rushing away into the night.

His fingers tightened around the handle of his gun. "Veronica!" he shouted again. He rushed into the road. He hadn't hit her, he knew he hadn't. *Please, don't let me have hit Veronica.*

She slowly rose from the other side of the road. She walked toward him with trembling steps.

He ran to her. He grabbed her, making sure they were out of the road in case that maniac came back, and he held her as tightly as he could. "What the hell happened?"

She was soaked. Her clothes were caked with mud, and her hair hung in wet clumps around her face. She shook against him, and her fear made the rage inside Jasper burn even brighter.

"H-he... That car, it forced me off the road."

*What?*

"Then th-the driver...he came back for me." Her arms flew up and wrapped around his neck. "He shot at me. He tried to kill me...and I was so scared that I wouldn't be able to get away."

*He shot at me.*

"Come on, sweetheart, let's get you out of here." He ran with her back across the road, put her inside his car, then did a quick check of the tires. They *should* be able to get out. If not, he'd claw their way out of that mud if he had to. Because he was getting her someplace safe.

He hurried back around to the driver's side, jumped in, gunned the engine. He pushed his foot down on the gas, and, at first, the wheels just spun.

"That's what happened to me," she whispered. Her hands were in her lap. Her shoulders hunched.

Clenching his jaw, he tried again. The tires found traction, and the vehicle lunged forward. He drove fast and hard, even as he yanked out his phone to call Logan. The other agent answered the call on the second ring.

"I'm on Hawkeye Road with Veronica." His words snapped out. "Some SOB in a black vehicle just took shots at her."

*"What?"*

"Classic car, the kind that would stick out in a place like this," Jasper said, his voice clipped. The length of the hood and trunk had been familiar to him. "No tags, but that car is going to be easy to track. Looked like an Impala."

"On it," Logan said. "You bringing her in?"

He slanted a fast glance at Veronica. *Someone had tried to kill her.* If he'd been just a few minutes later…

"I'll do whatever's necessary to keep her safe." Because in that one instant, when he'd seen her on the road, her beautiful face illuminated by his headlights, fear so heavy on her features, everything had changed for him.

This wasn't about a mission and not about a case.

It wasn't even about the poor men who'd lost their lives.

It was about Veronica. For him, she *was* the goal. Keeping her safe, keeping her alive and stopping the fool who thought that he'd hurt her.

*Not on my watch.*

Because until the EOD caught that guy, Jasper wasn't leaving Veronica's side.

# *Chapter Eleven*

She entered the makeshift EOD headquarters with slow steps. Veronica knew that she looked like hell, but she didn't care. She was pretty much just glad to be alive at this point.

Sydney's eyes widened when she caught sight of Veronica, and she hurried toward her. "Are you hurt?"

A few scrapes and bruises didn't qualify in Veronica's mind, so she shook her head. Jasper stood behind her, and she was far too conscious of him, and of the deadly look in his eyes. She'd made the mistake of looking into that lethal stare a few moments before. She'd never seen that level of rage before, not from anyone.

He'd been silent after that phone call to the other agent, but she'd felt his anger. When she looked into his eyes, she could see his fury.

Veronica cleared her throat. "I'm going to assume that my brother is still under guard."

Sydney nodded.

Veronica reached into her pocket and pulled out the flash drive. "Then you know he wasn't responsible for the shots taken at me. Someone else is hunting in this town. *Not Cale.* And this…this can prove his story about heading down to the Caribbean to work a case."

She handed the flash drive to Sydney.

A frown pulled Sydney's brows together. "Where'd you get this?"

"From Reed Montgomery's computer." She shrugged. The mud felt cold and hard on her skin. "So I tampered with the scene. Lock me up if you—"

"*No one* is locking you up," Jasper snarled immediately.

Sydney's eyes widened. "That's why the computer was smashed."

What? Veronica shook her head. "Look, I called earlier and told Jimmy what I'd found. He was supposed to tell—"

The doors burst open behind her. Wyatt rushed inside, his face haggard. "Veronica!" He grabbed her and pulled her into a crushing hug. "Oh, damn, when Logan got me on the radio and told me about the attack…" He pushed her back, stared down at her with blazing eyes. "Are you okay?"

She nodded. She wasn't going to let herself think too much about the bullet that had missed her head by about, oh, an inch.

Jasper clapped his hand down on Wyatt's shoulder and jerked him back. "Where were you?"

"I— What?" Wyatt frowned at him. "Kyle Jamison's house took a hit from the storm. A tree crashed into the side of his place. I went to see how he was, to make sure everything was all right."

"And where's your deputy?" Sydney asked him quietly.

Wyatt glanced back at her, brows rising. "Jimmy's out patrolling. With the storms still running through the area, we needed to make sure folks here were safe. That no one was stranded anywhere."

Stranded as she'd been. Stuck on the side of the road. Easy pickings.

No. Her shoulders straightened. *Not so easy.*

"Why are you checking on me?" Wyatt asked as his eyes suddenly narrowed. Then he looked over at Veronica. "Oh, no, you don't think that I—"

"Evidence has been destroyed," Sydney interrupted. "Evidence that only a few people in this town had access to."

"What kind of evidence?" Wyatt wanted to know as he yanked a hand through his wet hair.

"Reed Montgomery's computer. I think the killer smashed it to hell and back because he didn't want us to find…" Sydney held up the flash drive. "This."

He shook his head. "I haven't destroyed anything. Why would I care about Reed Montgomery's computer? I *want* you to catch any killers in my town.

This is a safe place." His voice dropped. "Or it was." Raindrops trickled down the side of his face. "I came to Whiskey Ridge so I could get away from all the death and violence. I sure never thought it would follow me here."

The door opened once more. Logan stepped inside. He swept a fast glance at Sydney, then at Jasper. The gaze he gave Wyatt held suspicion.

"I can't seem to locate your deputy," Logan said. "He won't answer his radio or his cell."

Wyatt's chin lifted. "Jimmy's probably just out of his car. Helping someone."

"Maybe." Logan's tone said he doubted that possibility.

Wyatt's gaze narrowed as he snapped to his full height. "You said someone *shot* at Veronica. Jimmy would never do that! The kid wants to keep everyone safe in this town. He'd have no reason to go after Veronica. She's—"

"Did he tell you that I called?" Veronica asked because she had to know this.

Everyone went silent.

She could hear the ticking of the clock on the desk in the lobby.

The lines on Wyatt's face deepened. Confusion clouded his eyes. "What call?"

That was the answer that she needed, and the one that she dreaded.

Jasper eased closer to her. "Why did you call the sheriff?"

"Because I didn't know your number." Her shoulder lifted in a sad shrug. *Jimmy.* She'd tutored him when he was in high school. Little Jimmy Jones. His dad had been killed in the military, and his mom had always struggled to make ends meet. Struggled... until Jimmy had been eighteen; then his mother had cut out of town and left him behind.

She'd never come back.

Taking a deep breath, Veronica said, "I called Wyatt because I thought he'd believe me about the evidence I'd found." She nodded toward Sydney's hand and the small drive that the agent had gripped in her fingers. "I knew the evidence was also on the computer that had been taken from the scene. A file that Reed had. By itself, it's not that much. I mean, it's a start, anyway. Bread crumbs that can help lead us to what's really happening."

"When did you call?" Sydney wanted to know.

"I... Jimmy didn't tell me that you called." Wyatt's voice was low now. She could see the suspicion in his gaze. When Jimmy had been left alone, Wyatt had stepped in. He tried to help the teen as much as he could. She knew Jimmy was a deputy because of Wyatt. Jimmy had wanted to be just like him.

*And like Cale.*

Cale had always been there for Jimmy, too. Teaching him to shoot. To hunt.

To…kill?

"When did you call?" Sydney repeated.

Veronica glanced at the clock on the desk. "About two hours ago."

"Right before the computer was smashed."

Jimmy? She just never would have suspected him. He still blushed when girls smiled at him. "The car that drove me off the road, it went back down Hawkeye, heading toward my house."

"Probably because he was going to search for the evidence," Jasper said, voice rumbling, "and when he couldn't find it there, he went back to make sure you didn't get a chance to tell anyone else about what you'd found."

Logan closed the distance between him and Sydney. "Can you get a GPS track going on his phone?"

She nodded. "As long as the phone's on." Then she turned away and headed out of the room.

Wyatt swore. "You're telling me…my own deputy…is the one who did all these murders? Him, and not Cale?"

Her gaze snapped up to Wyatt.

"Cale hasn't been cleared on anything yet," Logan said, eyes and voice both hard. "We're gonna find Jimmy. We'll bring him in, and then we'll see just what the hell is happening in this town."

For such a sleepy town, Whiskey Ridge sure had a lot of deaths.

Jasper's fingers curled around Veronica's wrist. "Let's get you cleaned up."

"I'm sure Sydney has some clothes she can borrow," Logan murmured. "You taking her to the motel?"

Jasper nodded. He tugged on Veronica's wrist. She didn't move. She was remembering that car, coming at her. At the time, she'd been so scared, but now... "Wyatt, didn't Jimmy buy an old car a few years back? One that he wanted to restore?"

"That black '67?" Wyatt gave a nod. "Yeah, he's been keeping it in his garage, but I think it's almost..."

He trailed off as he saw the tension on Jasper's face.

She thought about Jimmy's old car. About the long, heavy lines of the ride he'd loved so much. Then she said, sadly, "I'm pretty sure that's the car that ran me off the road."

Logan swore. Then he rushed to follow Sydney. "Syd, I need that GPS *now.*"

Because it looked as though they'd found the man who'd just tried to kill her, and it was one of the men who'd promised to protect and serve everyone in Whiskey Ridge.

VERONICA CAME OUT of the shower, dressed in a white terry cloth robe. Her hair trailed over her shoulders, and her skin was flushed.

She still looked too fragile. But he'd realized that the delicate appearance was only skin deep for Veronica.

The woman had a core of steel.

"When were you gonna tell me that you lifted that flash drive?" he asked her.

She paused at the threshold of the bathroom. Steam drifted around her. They were in his motel room. He had the door bolted, and he figured it was time they cleared the air between them.

Provided, of course, that he could keep his hands off her.

"I was going to get around to that," she murmured, "but there was the little matter of you getting shot, me finding out you were an EOD agent and, then, well, you arresting my brother."

"Yeah, the little matter of all that." He stalked toward her.

She tensed. "I thought I had the room to myself. You were supposed to wait outside while I showered."

"I'm not going anyplace. You were almost killed tonight." The memory had his heart racing. "Do you know what that did to me?"

She looked confused. As if she couldn't figure out why her death would matter to him.

He put his hands on her, right near her shoulders. She smelled fresh and clean and just looking at her made him ache. So the whole no-touching-her bit had lasted for all of five seconds. The woman made him weak.

"You were worried," she said, giving a little nod. "You're an agent, so your job is—"

"Forget the job." Anger thickened his voice. "This isn't about a job any longer. It's about you."

She blinked. "What?"

"I'm not on the EOD's side, okay? I'm not using you. I'm not trying to get information on your brother. I'm here, right now, because there is no other place on this whole earth that I'd rather be. I *want* to be with you."

"Jasper." Her gaze searched his.

What was she looking for? What emotion? What truth? Whatever it was, he sure as hell hoped that she found it.

"The case is between us, I get that. You think your brother's innocent? You think he's being set up by that deputy?"

"Yes." She breathed the words. "I do."

Such incredible faith. He wanted her to have that kind of faith in him.

"Then consider me on your side from here on out." The choice really was that simple to him. He couldn't keep ripping her apart by going after her brother. He'd resign from the EOD. He'd be with her.

If she wanted him.

"Wh-what are you saying?"

He had to kiss her. That little stutter got to him

every single time. His lips brushed hers, gentle, because he was determined to be, for now. "I'm saying that I have your back, always." Another kiss against her lips. "I'm saying that you can trust me to be there for you."

Her lips parted in surprise.

Another kiss. This time, his tongue dipped inside her mouth and tasted that sweetness.

"If your brother is being set up, we'll find the evidence that links Jimmy to the kills. We'll clear Cale."

*And if he isn't innocent...if Jimmy and Cale are somehow working together...*

He'd still be there for Veronica. From now on, he planned to be the man she needed him to be.

"Why?" she asked him softly. "Why are you changing your mind? Is it because of—"

"It's because of you." Simple. "I won't lose you." Not when she was everything that he'd ever been looking for his whole life.

Once, he'd told Logan that if a woman ever looked at him the way Logan's fiancée, Juliana, looked at that guy...well, Jasper had said that he'd hold as tight to that woman as he could. Jasper hadn't known a lot of love in his life, but he'd seen it in Juliana's gaze when she looked at Logan.

And, too late, he realized that he'd seen the same look in Veronica's eyes. Hope, trust, love—all of that had been in her eyes.

*I want that look again.* He'd work for it, do anything necessary, in order for her to look at him that way again.

"You wanted me once," he whispered against her mouth. "I can make you want me again."

Her hands rose, slowly, and settled lightly on either side of his jaw. Her stare was guarded now, but he could be patient. He could prove his worth to her.

"Jasper..."

He turned his head and pressed a kiss to her palm. "I can't lose you." How had she come to mean so much to him, so quickly? The image of her on that rain-soaked road would haunt him until he died.

"I'm not going anyplace," Veronica told him. She stepped closer to him, erasing the last bit of distance that separated them. "I want to be with you."

His control began to fracture. He kissed her again. Harder. Her hands dropped to his chest, smoothed over his skin. His fingers went to the belt of her robe, pulled the tie loose and slid inside to find smooth, naked skin.

But she pushed against him. "Jasper, your shoulder, your wound..."

"I'll hurt more if I can't have you." The need to take her again blazed through him. Death had been too close. He had to know that she was safe. Jasper wanted her body against his, and he wanted the pleasure to wipe away the fear that made him feel hollow inside.

And to think that some of his EOD buddies believed he was a man who didn't understand fear.

*I understand it now.*

Jasper kissed his way down her neck and enjoyed the shiver that slid over her body. Her hands were being so careful on him, but a little pain wasn't about to slow him down.

He led her to the bed. Kissed her, caressed the flesh that seemed to have been made just for his hands. Her nipples were tight, pink and he laved them with his tongue. She liked that. He could hear her pleasure in the moan that slipped from her lips. Good. Because he sure liked tasting her.

"I don't want to hurt you," she said again. Her hands were hesitant on him. He glanced up at her. Desire was warm in her eyes, and her flush had deepened.

He caught her hands, pushed them back over her head. Held them there with his left hand. "You'd only hurt me if you turned me away."

Her legs were open, parted slightly. He eased between her thighs and placed a kiss on her stomach.

*"Jasper?"*

His right hand caressed her flesh. He wanted her as aroused and eager as he was. Lust was a constant heat in his blood now, burning him from the inside out. But he wouldn't take, no, he wanted to give the pleasure to her.

Needed to see the pleasure on her face.

He pushed his fingers into her, stroked the most sensitive part of her body. Her hips arched up toward him. Eager. Not as eager as he was, not yet.

His fingers thrust again. He released her wrists, bent and tasted her.

She gasped out his name and that was the moment he'd been waiting for. The moment when pleasure and need merged for her.

After quickly taking care of the protection, he positioned his aroused length at the entrance of her body. Met her gaze. Saw the desire.

The...trust?

*Yes.*

He drove into her as his control shattered. She met every thrust, rising up with her hips, wrapping her arms around him—but not touching his shoulder. His Veronica. Always so careful.

So perfect for him.

His thrusts grew harder. Deeper. Her sex tightened around him, and he knew another release was close for her. His own climax was bearing down on him. He kissed her, because he wanted to taste her pleasure.

Then she was tensing beneath him as the wave of release hit her. Her sex contracted around him, and his climax ripped through Jasper, sending pleasure pouring through his body as he held her tightly beneath him.

They hadn't *just* had sex. He got that. He'd had

sex with plenty of women over the years. The pleasure he took with her, the way he felt…

*So much more.*

He stared down into her eyes. He could hear the drumming of his heartbeat filling his ears. She was everything he wanted, and he'd been a blind fool not to realize it sooner.

"Veronica."

She smiled up at him. "I didn't think it could get better." Her hand lifted. Traced a sensual path down his chest. "I was wrong."

His lips took hers.

A knock sounded at the door. A knock that he was very, very glad hadn't sounded about one minute sooner.

But Veronica's eyes still widened in alarm and her cheeks stained more with that lovely red. "Oh, no, do you think—"

"I think you should stay exactly where you are. It's just Logan or Sydney, coming with some extra clothes for you." He'd forgotten all about them until that moment.

He rose from the bed, pulled the covers over her and bent to grab the clothes that he didn't even remember ditching.

But Veronica was already hopping out of the bed. "I'm not staying here naked! What if they know— what if—"

Oh, they knew, all right. He was pretty sure that

Logan understood the hungry looks he'd been shooting at Veronica.

Unless he was very, very bad at reading people, there'd been a whole lot of desire and longing looks passing between Gunner and Sydney for months.

His team understood lust.

As for him, he was starting to understand love.

He headed for the door. After he checked through the peephole, he pulled it open. Because he didn't want to embarrass Veronica any more, he only opened the door a few inches.

Logan lifted a brow even as he also raised a small paper bag. "Some fresh clothes for your lady." The guy's voice was carefully expressionless.

Jasper tried to remember if he'd been…loud. Had he bellowed Veronica's name?

Logan's knowing look said, yep, he had. "Not a word to her," Jasper growled. No one would insult Veronica.

Logan nodded. "Wouldn't dream of it." But then his face hardened. "Sydney just got a hit on the deputy's cell phone. It turned on near Cale and Veronica's ranch."

The deputy must have doubled back. Maybe he was still looking for the evidence Veronica had taken from Reed's computer, hoping that Veronica didn't have it on her.

*Too bad. The EOD has the files.*

"We're going hunting." Logan cocked his head. "You in with us?"

Jasper looked over his shoulder at Veronica. She had belted the robe around her body again. She stared back at him with wide eyes.

"No," he said slowly as he turned back to face Logan. "I'm staying with Veronica. I don't want her alone." Not until he was exactly sure what they were dealing with. Deputy Jimmy Jones had looked like a scared kid the few times Jasper had seen him.

Jimmy *had* been at the police station the night it was torched. Wyatt had said the kid was in the back, and the flames and explosions had first started back there. And when Wyatt went looking for him, Jimmy had been gone.

*Gone because he'd been outside, killing witnesses?*

It sure looked that way.

*And Jimmy looked like a scared kid.*

"I thought you might say that…. Wyatt's inside the TH." Temporary Headquarters. Jasper knew the lingo. Logan continued. "He and Gunner are going to stay behind with Cale. Veronica could go there with them. She could—"

"No," Jasper said. He wasn't leaving her.

"Yes," Veronica responded at the same time. She grabbed the bag of clothes from Jasper's hand and pulled the door open even wider. "If you need backup, then Jasper's coming with you."

Logan glanced between them.

Her hand brushed against Jasper. "This is your job. You make sure that Jimmy comes in alive—he can come back and clear my brother."

Because proving her brother's innocence was the one thing that mattered most to Veronica.

"Logan has backup," Jasper said, still not willing to leave her. "Sydney's damn good at her job and—"

"It's a whole lot of land. It's a guy who knows the area," Veronica said, "and you're tracking him through a storm. If Sydney's found a link to him out at my ranch, you can't waste time. Go find him."

Because it was what she wanted, he nodded.

"We leave in five," Logan said as he stepped back.

Five minutes. Not long. Jasper shut the door. Pulled Veronica against him. "When I come back, you and I are gonna finalize some things."

She frowned up at him.

"The EOD." Jasper heaved out a breath as he tried to find the right words. "It doesn't have to be the only thing for me." He'd had another dream, one that had whispered through his mind for years.

The picket fence. A family.

Someone he loved.

"Finish this job," she whispered to him. "Come back, and we start fresh."

Sounded like one fine idea to him.

He kissed her and knew that he wouldn't, *couldn't* fail on this hunt.

HE WATCHED THE EOD agents leave. They thought they were so smart. Tracking him. Closing in. They didn't realize their mistake.

He'd been the one to turn on the cell phone so they could do their GPS tracking. He wanted them out on that ranch.

Because while the EOD was away, it gave him plenty of time to play.

He smiled and checked his weapon. Perfect.

They could search that ranch all night if they wanted. It would give him the chance he needed to take care of business.

He glanced down at his chest. At the stupid star near his heart. People acted as if that star was supposed to mean something to him.

It didn't mean a damn thing.

Money mattered. Getting paid for the jobs that he did. He'd been poor. He'd been pitied.

He'd never be that way again.

He'd found a way to get a whole new life, and to get that life, he'd just needed to *become* someone new. Cale wasn't so special. Not "Cale Lane," anyway. But "Striker"…he was special. People asked specifically for that mercenary when they went to Reed Montgomery.

Cale had balked at the jobs that weren't straight rescues. He'd never taken the hits. Even though those jobs paid the most cash.

So someone had taken the jobs for him. Reed had

been down with the switch. Morality hadn't been big with the guy, so Reed sure hadn't balked at lying about which mercenary actually took a job. People wanted Striker? Then they were told Striker handled the cases, even if someone else was actually doing the job. It had been the perfect situation.

But when Veronica just wouldn't give up on her hunt and those federal agents came to town, well, he hadn't been able to trust that Reed wouldn't turn on him.

So he'd eliminated Reed, just as he had the others.

For now...now it was time for the next step. Time to take over the "Striker" name once more and finish the job he'd started.

He'd been paid very, very well to take out EOD agents. Two more agents were on his hit list.

Gunner Ortez.

Sydney Sloan.

It seemed someone down in South America wanted those two out of the picture. The same someone who'd paid to have the other EOD agents eliminated. When he finished this job, he'd have a cool two million waiting in his Cayman Islands account.

There was a lot that a man could do with two million dollars. Hell, two million dollars could wash away so much blood.

He rubbed the star on his chest, checked his weapon once more and got ready to finish the job.

## Chapter Twelve

Inside the EOD team's headquarters, Veronica paced along the narrow hallway. She didn't see Gunner, but she knew he was just a short scream away. Not that she planned to scream.

*Jimmy? How could it have been Jimmy?* The idea still seemed wrong to her. Jimmy had been such a sweet guy. Lost, sad, hurt by his mother's abandonment, but he'd *cared* about Whiskey Ridge. He'd cared about her and Cale.

Hadn't he?

A man of the law, now being hunted. Soon enough, they'd find out what was happening with Jimmy. Soon—

Gunfire erupted, bursting from near the entrance of the headquarters. She tensed, then saw Wyatt rushing down the hallway to her. "It's Jimmy!" Sweat glistened on his forehead. "He took a shot at me when I got close to the front window! Saw him…" He huffed out a breath. "For just a second… Fired back…" His fingers clenched around hers. "I think I hit him."

Footsteps thundered behind her. She looked over her shoulder. Gunner was there, with his gun out, and his face was a hard mask. "What's happening?" he demanded.

"Jimmy's outside," she said. "Wyatt thinks that he shot the deputy."

Gunner's hold tightened on his weapon. "Take her to the back. I'll check it out."

Wyatt's fingers were trembling. How must he feel? To have shot Jimmy.

"I nearly raised him…" Wyatt whispered as he shook his head. "That boy…how could he do this?" He pulled her down the hallway. "How?" Pain deepened his voice.

More stumbling steps and they were near the end of the hallway. The room that housed Cale was to the right.

"Go on in there," Wyatt said with a nod toward the door. "Stay with Cale until we make sure Jimmy is…" Wyatt's breath blew out on a rough sigh. "Just stay with him." Then he was gone. Rushing back down the hallway.

She opened the door. The handle turned easily beneath her fingers. She would have thought that Gunner had locked the room, but maybe her brother had—

The room was empty. Cale was gone. The slats of wood had been pried off the window.

Gunfire blasted once more.

JASPER AND LOGAN HAD their weapons out. They were scanning the area around Veronica's ranch. So far, there were no signs of Jimmy.

Not yet.

"The front door's open," Logan whispered.

Jasper nodded to show he'd heard. Then he gave a quick gesture with his hand. He'd go in first, and Logan could follow for cover.

One, two...

By three, he was in the house. And the house had most definitely been searched. Ransacked. Not just Veronica's room this time. Not just Cale's room.

Everything had been destroyed.

Was the guy still in there? Only one way to find out. Another fast hand gesture, and he and Logan swept through the kitchen. Sydney had her weapon out now, too, and she flanked them. Room by room, they searched.

Downstairs.

Upstairs.

Broken furniture. Overturned chairs.

But no Jimmy Jones.

Jasper peered down from Veronica's window. "He could be in any of those buildings." Just like before. Only this time, the guy was watching them, not Veronica.

"If he's out there, why hasn't he taken us out?" Sydney asked. "He could have gotten shots off when we came on the porch."

"Maybe our cover was too good. He didn't have a clean shot," Logan said instantly. "Maybe—" He broke off, frowning, then pulled his phone out of his back pocket. The phone made no sound, but Jasper knew the device would be emitting a small vibration. "It's Gunner." Logan put the phone to his ear. "Area isn't secure yet. We're—"

Jasper saw his eyes widen.

"When? Damn it, yes, we're on the way." He shoved the phone back into his pocket. "Gunner says we aren't going to find the deputy out here. He's back in town, shooting at Wyatt."

"He lured us away," Sydney said with a shake of her head even as they all raced for the stairs. "That guy wanted to separate us so he could attack better. He left his phone for us to track."

Now he was heading in to take out Cale. And Veronica. They rushed out of the front door. The porch creaked beneath their feet.

But then they heard the peal of a ringing cell phone, a sound that came from within the house. Jimmy's phone? Sydney glanced back at the house. "Why..." Then her eyes widened. "The bomb at the sheriff's station—it was triggered by a cell! He could be doing it again! *Run!*"

But there wasn't time to run. The house exploded behind them. The force of the blast sent Jasper flying into the air, and then he hit the ground with a bone-jarring thud.

VERONICA RUSHED BACK down the hallway. There was no more gunfire. Just silence. She crouched low, not wanting to make a target, and turned the corner that would take her back to the small lobby.

"Wyatt?" Veronica whispered. He was bent near the front desk.

He turned around, eyes widening. He had his phone in his hand. "I can't get Logan and the others." Worry hardened his words. "No one's answering."

She swallowed over the lump in her throat. "And Cale's gone."

Wyatt tensed. "What?" Then, suddenly, Wyatt was right in front of her, grabbing her arm and pulling her close. "Hell, he's supposed to be cuffed back there."

"The handcuffs were on the floor. The room was empty. *He's gone.* H-he must have picked the lock and managed to pry the boards off the window." The EOD had underestimated him. Her brother had gotten out of plenty of tight spots over the years. As if that little room would have held him for long.

Wyatt glanced over his shoulder. "Is that Jimmy out there shooting at us...or Cale?"

Shock squeezed her heart. "B-but you said... Jimmy..."

"I never saw the shooter." His confession was a rough rasp. "I just assumed..." He shook his head. "Never mind. We have to get out there. Gunner needs to know who he's facing." His gaze penned hers. "You stay low and you move fast, got it?"

She had it, all right. But she'd feel better if she had a weapon. If she had *something*. Her gaze flew around the room. The filing cabinets. The desk.

She swiped out with her hand, grabbing the small weapon that probably wouldn't do her a bit of good.

Then she followed Wyatt. She stayed down. She moved fast. Just as he'd told her. Just as...

"Get in," Wyatt ordered roughly.

They were at his patrol car. He was trying to push her into the back.

There was no gunfire. No sign of Gunner or Cale or Jimmy.

And Wyatt was sweating so much. From fear. From adrenaline. From...something more?

Her fingers were curled around the small letter opener that she'd grabbed from the desk. "You didn't say we were going to leave Gunner."

"I don't *see* him." His gaze darted to the left. To the right. "So the only thing we can do is go to the ranch and try to find the others. Then we'll come back."

"But Jimmy could get away. Cale could—"

He pushed her toward the backseat. "We don't have time to argue, Veronica! Let's go!"

But she hesitated. Something just felt wrong.

*"Veronica!"*

Cale's voice. She started to smile then. It was going to be all right. It was—

Wyatt spun at Cale's shout. He brought up his gun and fired.

She screamed when her brother fell back. Screamed—and shoved that letter opener into Wyatt's shoulder. The bellow of pain was his, but she was already moving, trying to jerk his gun away. He was strong, though, far stronger than she'd realized, and he shoved her, sending her tumbling into the back of his patrol car. She lunged up in an instant.

And found herself staring down the barrel of his gun.

"Didn't want it to be like this," Wyatt muttered, with a shake of his head. "Not for you. I had other plans for you."

"Wyatt?"

Another gunshot rang out. It ricocheted off the open patrol car door. Wyatt swore and dropped low. She rushed forward, but he slammed the door, sealing her inside.

There were no handles on the back door. No way

to lower the windows. A wire cage separated her from the front seat.

More gunfire erupted. One bullet hit Wyatt in the shoulder. He was snarling and lifting his gun, spinning around and seeming to fire right up into the air. Then he was lunging into the front of the patrol car. Revving the car's engine and racing away. Veronica was yelling for him to stop. But he wasn't.

She spun back to look behind her. Cale was trying to sit up. His chest was soaked with blood and his hand was up, as if he were reaching for her.

Gunner ran up behind Cale, a gun still gripped in the agent's hand. Gunner lifted that gun, as if he'd fire.

Then his gaze locked on hers.

*Help me.*

Gunner didn't fire.

Wyatt left them with a scream of his tires.

JASPER PUSHED TO his feet. The house was an inferno, blazing out of control. The house that Veronica had loved.

"That's how he did it at the station," Sydney murmured. She didn't seem to be aware that a one-inch gash was dripping blood down her cheek. "He had the bomb already wired. He knew we were bringing in the kidnappers. He just had to press a few buttons, make one call."

And the station had exploded.

Sydney yanked out her phone. Dialed fast. Then, "Gunner, listen, the ranch has just—" She broke off, inhaling sharply. Her stare was on Jasper and he saw the horror in her eyes. Saw the faintest tremble of her lower lip, and he knew the news she'd gotten had been bad.

*Veronica.*

"But…but you're all right?" Sydney whispered uncertainly.

Sydney was never uncertain.

Jasper took a step forward. Logan was on his feet now and they were both closing in on Sydney even as the house burned. "We'll be right there," she said. "But—what? What has Cale done?"

*He wouldn't hurt Veronica. Cale would never…*

Sydney lowered her phone. "Logan, use your pull. Call D.C. and get them to send some county backup over to us *now*. The deputy's still missing, and Veronica…" Her gaze cut back to Jasper. "She's been taken."

Jasper was already shaking his head because that just wasn't an option. She couldn't be taken by anyone. She couldn't be hurt. He needed her too much and—

"It was the sheriff," Sydney said. "Gunner told me the guy shot Cale and then Wyatt forced Veronica into the back of a patrol car. He took off, going hell fast, but Cale's following him. I guess a bullet can't slow him down for long."

Everything seemed to slow down for Jasper. Even the heat of the flames seemed to die away.

*Wyatt forced Veronica into the back of a patrol car.*

"He's dead," Jasper whispered.

Sydney flinched. She put the phone back to her ear. "Gunner, do you have Cale within sight? I know he took the motorcycle but..." Her worried stare wasn't leaving Jasper.

Only he could barely see her. In his mind, he just saw Veronica. Scared. He didn't want her to be scared.

He'd said that he would keep her safe.

And he was damn well gonna do it.

Sydney was off the phone now, but Logan had yanked out *his* phone to call for backup. Jasper wasn't about to let any more time waste. "Tell me that you can track Cale," he said to Sydney. Sometimes the EOD would put tracking chips under the skin of certain witnesses, witnesses who were in danger of being abducted or killed. Logan's Juliana had been one of those witnesses. That tracking device had saved her life. Maybe—

Sydney shook her head.

*No.*

"The sheriff took her," Jasper gritted out. The man had been right there, with them every step of the way. He should have known. He should have suspected.

But he'd been focused on the mission, on capturing Cale. Then he'd been blindsided by Veronica.

*I'm coming, Veronica. I won't let you down.*

"The sheriff knows every inch of this county," Logan said, coming back to them. Flames crackled behind them. "He's gonna have the advantage on us." The guy could just disappear. Or just dump Veronica's body someplace and *then* vanish.

Jasper turned away, began walking at first, then flat-out running toward the car.

"Jasper!" Logan called out.

Jasper didn't stop. He jumped in the vehicle. Sydney had another car. He wasn't abandoning the other agents. He just wasn't waiting. *Veronica needs me.* Jasper jerked the keys in the ignition, and the engine snarled to life.

Logan's hand slammed against the driver's-side door. "You don't even know where to look," Logan snapped. "Let us get some intel together and—"

"You get your intel. Get Sydney to run all those phone searches and GPS hunts like she does." His fingers clenched around the wheel. "I'll go back to town and tear every building down if I have to. I won't let her—"

His phone rang. He grabbed it instantly. "Veronica!"

A faint laugh rolled into his ear. "No, but she's close," Jasper was told.

Then he heard Veronica scream.

He almost crushed the phone in his hands.

"Want to see her, Ranger? Then you ditch those other EOD jerks," Wyatt told him, voice grating. "You lose every single one of them, and you get yourself out to the old ranch at the end of Derby Road."

Derby Road? He had no idea where that road was, but he'd load the name into the GPS and find that ranch.

"You've got twenty minutes to get there, or I'll put a bullet into Veronica."

Jaw clenching, Jasper looked back up at Logan. Logan was his friend, his team leader. He knew the way situations like this were supposed to go down.

Except this wasn't just a case. Not a normal mission. It was Veronica.

"I love her," he said, the only thing that he *could* say. Logan would know who'd just made that call.

Logan's gaze told him that he understood, but Logan shook his head. "Give us the location. You need some backup. We can help!"

Jasper shook his head. "Get away from the car."

Logan's jaw clenched. But he jumped back.

Jasper raced away from that burning ranch house. He couldn't think of anything, anyone else just now…only Veronica.

"HE'S GOING AFTER her?" Sydney asked softly as she watched the car rush down the narrow highway.

The flames burned behind them, the heat seeming to scorch her flesh.

"Wyatt called him. I'm betting the SOB told him that if he brought backup, the girl would die."

Wasn't that always the way it was.

Sydney pulled out her phone. Scrolled through the carefully designed apps she had in her system—applications that she'd designed herself. "How long of a head start do you think Jasper wants?"

Because Jasper would know that the EOD would be able to follow him. As long as his phone was still on, they could track him.

Maybe Jasper was worried that Wyatt had a partner—that missing deputy—who might be watching them right now. So he wanted to make it look as if he were going in alone. Or maybe he just was thinking with his heart and not his head. Either way, the EOD never left a teammate on his own.

Never.

"Ten minutes," Logan said with a nod. His gaze was still on Jasper's fleeing vehicle. "That'll give him time to get to his destination, go in and take out the sheriff."

Ten minutes. Plenty of time for an EOD agent to complete a mission. Only...

It was also plenty of time for a man to die.

"The sheriff got the drop on three other agents," she reminded Logan, trying to keep her voice calm. "He's not your average killer." That fact should have turned up in her search. Where had the guy gotten all of his training?

"Make it five minutes," Logan said, and she could see the tension that had tightened his face. "Make sure Gunner's on the move with the same intel, too. We want to give Jasper as much cover as we can."

In the distance, she could finally hear the scream of a fire truck's siren. Volunteers, had to be for a town this size, but with one phone call, Logan had gotten them mobilized. The EOD had some pretty powerful strings.

Would the EOD be strong enough to save one of its own? "Five minutes," she repeated, and punched in the button for Gunner. They *would* save Jasper and Veronica. They hadn't lost one of the Shadow Agents yet, and they weren't about to start now.

THE OLD RANCH on Derby Road was just as Veronica remembered it. Sagging roof, busted windows, a wooden gate that was barely standing. The place had been in disrepair for over ten years.

Since before Jimmy's mother had left the kid alone there.

The patrol car braked to a stop. Veronica had been yelling when Wyatt was on the phone. She'd tried to tell Jasper to stay away.

*Because it's a trap.*

As soon as Wyatt saw him, she knew the sheriff

would take aim at Jasper, just as the man had taken aim at her brother.

Her fingers curled over the wire caging that separated her from the front seat. "Is Jimmy dead?"

Wyatt jumped, then whirled toward her. "Why would you think that?" He shook his head. "I've always taken care of Jimmy."

*The way you've taken care of me?* "Where is he?"

Wyatt's breath eased out on a low sigh. "Don't worry, you'll be seeing Jimmy soon enough."

The words sounded like a threat. Probably because they were. "You shot my brother."

Wyatt's eyes bored into hers. "Your brother's a killer, Veronica. Cold-blooded. Soulless."

No, Wyatt was the cold-blooded one. "I—I heard what you said to Jasper—"

"Don't worry, I'm not killing you…yet."

But he would. As soon as he was finished using her as bait.

She licked lips that had gone desert dry. Veronica knew she had to get away from him. Had to stop him, before he hurt someone else that she cared about. Or before he just killed her.

But then Wyatt was climbing out of the driver's seat, coming back toward her and opening her door. "If you fight me, I'll shoot you. Jasper won't be able to tell if you're alive or dead from a distance."

She couldn't even speak in response to the brutal words. *This* was the real Wyatt? He'd had weekly dinners at the ranch. Spent Christmas with her and Cale.

*Now he's going to kill me.*

"Don't fight, Veronica," he warned her as he reached inside the car and locked his hands around her wrists.

She didn't fight him. But she started to plan.

Then she was in front of him. She tipped back her head to stare up at his face. A monster shouldn't have such a normal face. You should be able to see the evil. It shouldn't have hid so easily behind kind eyes.

"I always liked you, Veronica." Wyatt's words were soft, tinged with a hint of regret. "Cale should have made certain you stayed out of this mess."

"C-Cale didn't bring me into it. I went looking for him."

"Because you're loyal." He was too close. She wanted to swing at him, but she had a really crummy punch. Cale had said that was her weakness, but...

*"Everybody has a strength. Everybody has a weakness. Your strength, Ronnie, is that you look weak. Use that. Never let 'em see your real strength, not until it's time to attack."*

"I admire loyalty." He stepped away from her. A faint breeze stirred the hair at her nape. "Do you think you ever could've been loyal to me?"

She didn't know what to say. The man was crazy, and at any moment, she expected him to snap and just shoot her. Her gaze darted to the left and tension had her body stiffening.

The long, black car. The one that had run her off the road.

"Jimmy's car." Now Wyatt sounded sad. "You and Jasper got the description right."

"You were driving. Not Jimmy."

"You had the flash drive." Just that fast, anger whipped in his words. "The files should have been gone, but you *had* them."

She wouldn't let him see her fear. "I gave the flash drive to Sydney. She has the evidence that can clear my brother."

He growled. "It wasn't just the damn drive. It was all those pictures you kept talking about. Pictures from Cale's time in the military."

Her breath caught. The pictures had linked Cale to Reed, but they hadn't been much help for anything else.

"Was I in those pictures, Veronica?" Wyatt asked her softly.

She'd known that Wyatt had served in the army, but Veronica shook her head.

"You wouldn't be lying now, would you? Because those pictures…I won't let them ruin things for me. Cale served with me when we had demolitions training."

Demolitions…the bomb at the sheriff's station…

"Reed was with us then. That's how I knew he

was in the business. With all those agents still circling town, I can't have those pictures turning up."

"Y-you weren't in the pictures," she whispered, and it was the truth. He wasn't.

He exhaled slowly. "Well, then, I guess I just blew your house to hell for no reason. But, hey…" Now he flashed her a smile that held the edge of insanity. "Better safe than sorry, right?"

How had he hid his darkness? *"Why?"*

"For money, of course. Isn't that why people do most of the things in this world?" He rolled his shoulders. "But when the smoke clears, it won't be me who gets blamed for the crimes." His smile had dimmed. "Folks will say Jimmy blew up your house. Just like he destroyed my station. Then, torn up by what he'd done, Jimmy came back here and shot himself."

Her knees buckled. Wyatt grabbed her, held her steady.

Her lashes had lowered. She put her hands on his stomach, acting as if she needed balance.

*Don't show him your strength.*

"You said you took care of him."

"And I did." A pause. "Pity that kid never appreciated the lessons I taught him."

She shoved against his chest, and because he hadn't been expecting the move, it was easy for her to grab the gun he'd had holstered at his waist. Her hand snapped up, fingers locked around the weapon. *"Get away from me!"*

Wyatt blinked at her in surprise, and then his gaze dipped down to the gun that was inches away from him. "You shouldn't have done that."

"And you shouldn't have been a cold-blooded killer, so I guess we've both screwed up, huh?"

Wyatt flashed his smile once more. The sight chilled her. "Veronica, you've got more steel in your spine than I thought."

She'd show him steel, or rather, lead, when she shot a bullet into his chest. "Why do you want Jasper out here? Is he next on your hit list?" she whispered. "Another EOD agent that you've been paid to take out, one that you were supposed to link back to Cale?"

"Give me the gun, Veronica."

She couldn't back up because the patrol car was behind her. She couldn't move forward because Wyatt was blocking her path. "Get *back!*" she yelled.

He didn't get back. "You won't shoot me." So confident.

"Yes. I will." She was just as confident. "You were the one on the side of that road, shooting at me. Not Jimmy. *You.*"

He still had that slight smile on his lips. "How are you gonna prove that?"

"When Jasper gets h-here, he'll take you into custody. We'll find Jimmy. We'll get proof that you were behind everything and not—"

"Your Jasper's gonna die today. Cale's gonna die. They'll both go out in a gun battle as they try to save you." He gave a slow shake of his head. "But they aren't gonna save you, either."

Her heartbeat thundered in her ears. "I can save myself."

"No, you can't." Then he lunged for her.

She shot him. Didn't so much as hesitate. The gun blasted and her ears rang and the bullet slammed into his stomach.

His eyes widened in surprise as he looked down at the blossoming red on his shirt. Wyatt stumbled back, and she took that opportunity to slam her shoulder into him and knock him to the ground. Then she ran as fast as she could—not toward the old highway, but toward that long, black car that sat near the side of the crumbling house. Jimmy's car. Because she could just see the top of Jimmy's head in the car.

She yanked open the passenger door. "Jimmy!" He was inside, his hands and feet tied. And his chest was bleeding. So much blood. She reached for him, yanking the ropes free that bound his wrists. He'd taken a shot straight to the chest.

"Ms. Ver...on..." He tried to speak, but the words just came out as a rasp.

"It's okay. I'm going to help you, Jimmy." He'd

escaped this hellhole of a ranch once. She wasn't letting him die there. She tried to slide him over to the passenger side. Wyatt had left the kid behind the steering wheel. She'd move him over and drive them both out of there. She rushed around to the driver's side and—

*"Veronica!"*

Her head jerked to the left at that bellow. Wyatt was on his feet. He had reached into his patrol car. Pulled out— Oh, no, that was a shotgun in his hands. He'd gotten a shotgun, and he was pointing it at her.

She jumped into Jimmy's car. The back window shattered behind her. Ducking, she searched under the seat for the keys. Nothing. Not there. Not…

"I've got the keys, Veronica!" Wyatt called out. "Why don't you come and get them?"

She wasn't coming for them…because she didn't need them.

She grabbed the wires underneath the dash. Yanked down hard. Twisted them. Jerked the ends together and…

The motor sparked to life. During all of Cale's car talks with her, he'd made sure to teach her a few tricks over the years.

"Hold on," Veronica whispered to Jimmy. Then she slammed the vehicle into Reverse.

She glanced up, just in time to see Wyatt standing behind the car. Aiming his shotgun at her. She slammed her foot down harder on the accelerator.

The back bumper rammed into Wyatt even as he fired the gun. The blast had her jumping and yanking the wheel to the right. The car swerved, but beneath her sweat-slick hands, she managed to keep the vehicle steady. She glanced around wildly. Wyatt had disappeared or maybe—maybe she'd just taken him out and he was on the ground. Either way, she wasn't about to get out of the car and check. She was just getting her and Jimmy the hell out of there.

She shifted, preparing to head straight out on that bumpy drive, when a shotgun was shoved into the open driver's-side window. The shotgun pressed right against her head. "Get out or die right there," Wyatt snarled.

She froze.

"Get. Out."

Slowly, carefully, she eased from the car. Jimmy whimpered beside her. "No...Ms. Ver...on..."

The right side of Wyatt's face was covered in blood. His stomach was soaked red. But the guy was standing strong. The second she cleared the car, he jerked her against him. "Guess what?" he whispered as he put the barrel of that shotgun under her chin.

She didn't want to guess anything. She wanted to see Cale once more. She wanted to see Jasper. *Jasper.* She wanted him so much.

"It's empty."

It took a moment for the words to register. Then

she heard Wyatt's smug laugh. "You could've gotten away."

She wasn't looking at him. Barely felt the shotgun as it was yanked away and dropped in the dirt. Her gaze was on the driveway before her. A blue car was fishtailing as it swerved down that jagged road. And to the right, a motorcycle was coming right out of the overgrown brush.

Wyatt bent and pulled a small pistol from the holster on his ankle. "This is the moment," he said in her ear, "the life-or-death moment that everyone talks about but so damn few get to experience. I'll give this moment to you."

Jasper had just jumped out of the blue car. He was closing in on her. He had a gun gripped in his hands. "Let her go!"

Cale was shoving away from the motorcycle. He was armed, too, with a small gun that he had pointed right at Wyatt. "There's no way out for you, Wyatt! Get away from my sister!"

"Neither one of them will shoot," Wyatt whispered in her ear. "Because they're scared they'll hit you." He'd positioned the gun under her chin, holding it in exactly the same spot he'd put the shotgun. Only this time, she was betting this gun was loaded and ready to kill. "Or maybe they're just afraid I'll pull the trigger."

Her head was tilted back against him as she tried

to get away from that weapon. But there was no place to go. She couldn't get free.

The two men she loved most were closing in. Just about ten feet away from her now. Why was Wyatt letting them come so close?

*Because he's going to kill them both.* Her breath stilled. That was Wyatt's plan. He was using her to lure Jasper and Cale closer. And when they were close enough, he'd shoot one man, and the other still wouldn't fire back because he'd be afraid of shooting *her*.

*Neither one of them will shoot.*

Wyatt had that part right. But he was still wrong about one thing. "I can save myself," she whispered again. But it wasn't just about surviving this mess. She was ready to risk her life for the men that she loved.

*You don't risk your life for nothing.* Cale's number three rule. But this risk wasn't for nothing. It was for everything. For their lives.

She looked into Cale's eyes. Her brother was only about seven feet away now. She'd never seen such fear in his eyes.

"It's going to be okay, Ronnie," Cale told her. "You'll make it out of this."

Would he?

Her gaze darted to Jasper. No fear there. Just desperate determination. An intensity that would have scared her if she didn't know him so well. He was looking at Wyatt, and promising death. "Get your hands *off* her!" Jasper snarled.

"You messed this up for me," Wyatt yelled right back at him. "You weren't supposed to be EOD. You were just supposed to be a mercenary. Expendable...*dead*."

And she *knew* that Wyatt was going to shoot at Jasper first. Because Wyatt would rely on Cale's bond with Veronica. A brother wouldn't shoot at his sister, right? Jasper was the variable threat that Wyatt would want to eliminate first.

*I won't let you kill him.* She'd just found Jasper. He wasn't dying.

"He's not...expendable," she said, her voice flat and cold. "You are." Then she drove her elbow into his ribs as hard as she could. He jerked behind her, startled, and the gun slipped away from her chin, moving about two inches.

That two inches was all that she needed.

She leaped toward Jasper even as she screamed, "Shoot him, Cale!"

Jasper's arms were reaching for her. She tried to push him back because she was afraid Wyatt would take the shot. But Jasper was too strong. Always so strong. He twisted, protecting her, using his body as a shield.

Gunfire exploded behind her. Once. Twice.

Then she felt the hard jerk that knocked Jasper— *as a bullet hit him?*

"Jasper!"

They were both on the ground. Jasper was on top of her, covering her with his body. But no, she'd wanted to protect *him*.

"Jasper?" she whispered.

His head lifted. He stared down at her with so much emotion blazing in his eyes that she couldn't speak again. "Stay here," he whispered, and he rose.

He turned his back on her, and she saw the blood. The bullet had hit him. A bullet that she'd tried so hard to stop.

She pushed to her knees.

Cale was standing over Wyatt's prone body. Cale's legs were braced apart and his gun was trained on the sheriff. Only Wyatt wasn't moving.

"He's dead!" Cale shouted. "Take care of Veronica!"

Jasper turned toward her, but she was already wrapping her arms around him. His body trembled against hers, and that tremble scared her more than anything else. Jasper was always strong. Always so in control. Always...

He kissed her. Hard, desperate. His arms wrapped around her so tightly that her ribs hurt. She didn't care. She held him just as tightly, clinging to him as fiercely as she could.

It had been too close. *Too* close. In those terrible moments, she'd realized...*I don't want to be without him.*

"Scared me," Jasper rasped against her mouth.

She could feel his blood on her fingertips. He was still scaring her. "Jasper, you're hurt." Serious understatement. The bullet hadn't come out; she could see that much for herself. It was still lodged in his back.

"Won't ever…lose you…"

"No," she whispered at once. "You won't. Jasper—"

"Love you…Veronica Lane…"

She couldn't breathe. "Jasper, I love you, too!" She stood on her toes to kiss him again and that was when they fell. Jasper's body seemed to crumble against hers, and they hit the ground. "Jasper?"

She tried to shake him, to get him back up, but his eyes were closed. He wasn't moving.

*"Jasper!"*

But he wasn't answering. She remembered the blood on his back. The bullet. And Jasper's skin seemed to be losing its warmth. The warmth that had been there to banish the chill and the worry that had cloaked her for so long. That warmth was fading now.

Desperate, she looked up. "Cale! Cale, *help me!*"

Her brother rushed to her side. Behind them, she heard the growl of more motors as other cars rushed to the scene. She didn't look back at those cars. Didn't look at anyone or anything but Cale and Jasper. Cale's face was grim as he looked down at her lover. Jasper was pale, too pale.

"Don't leave me," Veronica whispered to Jasper, and she pressed a kiss to his lips. "Don't."

Her fingers curled around his. His lashes seemed to flutter. No, maybe that was just the wind. Not him, not...

"I...won't..." Jasper whispered.

Her breath choked out. Jasper had just made her a promise.

She wouldn't let him break it.

Sydney and Logan ran to his side. Veronica kept her hold on Jasper's wrist, and even when the EMT crew came, she didn't let go.

She would never let go of the man she loved.

Death could just wait. She wasn't done with Jasper Adams yet. Not by a long shot.

## Chapter Thirteen

Not many people bothered to come to the funeral. Seemed as if the folks in Whiskey Ridge were too betrayed and shocked by the actions of Wyatt Halliday to be able to forgive him, even in death.

But Veronica was there. Standing silently beside the grave. To her right, the young deputy was looking as if he'd seen a few better days.

The poor kid probably had. But at least Jimmy Jones was alive, thanks to Veronica. He could look forward to a whole lot of better days to come.

"I've seen the way you look at my sister," Cale said, the words whisper soft.

Jasper turned his head to meet Cale's hard stare. The man hadn't really changed that much in the past ten years. A fierce fighter, a loving older brother and a man who would kill in order to protect the ones he cared for in this world.

The funeral service was over. The few mourners were turning away.

Jasper shifted his stance lightly. That bullet of

Wyatt's had come close to his spine. A little too close for comfort. He'd taken six hits before and been able to keep walking. But that one bullet had almost taken him out.

He'd been in the hospital for two weeks. Wyatt's service had been delayed while Uncle Sam finished the investigation on the EOD murders.

The case was closed now, mostly, anyway.

"I still think she's too good for you," Cale muttered. He'd only been in the hospital for a day; the wound he'd received had been easy to patch.

"You're never gonna think anyone is good enough for her," Jasper said. But Cale's words were true. Hell, Jasper *knew* he wasn't good enough.

Veronica turned and smiled at him.

*But I don't care if I'm not good enough.* She wanted him. Somehow, that woman actually wanted him.

"What kind of life will you give her?" Cale pressed. "Always running off on the next mission, leaving her behind. That's what I've already done to her. Our parents left us. Then *I* left her, again and again, on the missions that called me." His voice tightened. "Missions that I could have turned away, but I didn't."

Because the man was a soldier at heart. The missions had called, and he had answered.

Jasper had been like that once, too. But things

were different for him now. In his missions, he'd always been looking for something...

Someone.

Veronica was walking toward him.

*I found her.*

"There won't be any more missions," Jasper said as he glanced back at Cale.

Cale frowned. "What?"

Instead of repeating himself, Jasper said, "I was wondering, are you interested in selling your part of the ranch?"

"What ranch? I never fixed the place up and it's blown to hell now."

Maybe. Or maybe it was just ripe for starting over. Maybe this town was the place that he needed. Veronica was the woman he needed.

She was right in front of him now. They hadn't been able to talk alone yet. Too many doctors. Too many EOD agents.

But he'd have her all to himself. Soon.

"I was told there's a briefing today," she said, raising her brows. "Do we go to headquarters?"

Headquarters. That run-down building that the EOD had claimed. The new sheriff would need a better central location. The new sheriff in town would need a whole lot.

Jasper nodded.

He noticed that Jimmy was just a few steps behind Veronica. The kid had been shadowing her.

Whenever he looked at Cale or Jasper, he turned ghost-white.

They'd be getting rid of his fear at that briefing. The EOD would share its findings, and the case would be over.

Jasper glanced over at the closed casket.

No more murders in Whiskey Ridge. No more fear.

Time to start fresh.

*If* Veronica would have him.

THE TICKING OF the clock on the small desk was way too loud. Every tick had Veronica tensing. She knew this meeting was necessary, but the last time she'd been in this building, well, she'd been scared to death.

*Almost as scared as I am now.*

Jasper was out of the hospital. Finally. The doctors hadn't let her see him once he'd been wheeled back to the O.R. She hadn't been family, and there'd been cops and agents all around him. She'd been pushed back. Veronica remembered pacing the floor of that narrow waiting room again and again. Then she'd broken down and slipped back into the recovery room. Gotten some scrubs, acted as though she belonged and seen for herself that Jasper was going to be all right.

She'd even kissed him back there, until a stunned

nurse had appeared, but that nurse had taken pity on Veronica and let her stay a little longer.

*I just want to be with him a little longer.*

Only her time was up now. The EOD agents had closed their case. They'd be leaving town, moving, as Jasper had once told her, as soundlessly as shadows as they slipped from Whiskey Ridge.

From her life.

"Cale Lane," Logan said, drawing Veronica's attention as the agent looked at her brother, "on behalf of the EOD, we want you to know that you've been cleared in this investigation." The words were formal, real official sounding.

Cale just raised a brow. "I kind of figured that, you know, when you didn't throw my butt in jail."

Sydney's lips twitched.

"Wyatt was pretending to be me," Cale continued, voice harder now, "and Reed Montgomery was the one giving him the cases."

Logan nodded. "From the intel that Sydney recovered—courtesy of your sister's flash drive— Reed let his contact in South America believe that you were actually taking the EOD hits. Striker was assigned the jobs, but it was actually Wyatt who tracked and eliminated the targets."

*Targets.* Veronica swallowed. That was such a cold, clinical way of referring to people.

"I told Wyatt that I was getting out of the business, that I was gonna stay at the ranch more with

Veronica." Cale glanced her way. "That must have been when he decided he could use my name."

"He planned to make you disappear," Jasper said. She jerked at his voice, way too sensitive toward him. "You were supposed to be taken out on that case in the Caribbean, but you went off the radar."

"Because I know a trap when I walk into one," Cale muttered with a sad shake of his head.

"But when you vanished—" Now Sydney was talking. Gunner stood, still and silent, behind her. "—Wyatt knew he'd have to find you and kill you in order to tie up all the loose ends. He left evidence at his kill scenes, evidence to tie you to the crimes."

"The guy picked up a lot of crime-scene knowledge from his time in the Dallas P.D.," Logan said, tapping his fingers against a nearby file. "Seems he was even dating an M.E. for a while. I'm guessing she shared some tools of the trade with him."

And Wyatt had used that knowledge to plant evidence against her brother.

"If the EOD caught Cale, Wyatt was counting on the evidence he'd left behind to send you to jail," Sydney said. Her gaze was on Cale. "And if that didn't work…" Now Sydney's green stare drifted to Veronica. "Well, Wyatt knew that there was one thing that would always bring you back to Whiskey Ridge."

Veronica hated being bait.

"Wyatt just had to bide his time and watch Veronica." Jasper's jaw tightened as he gritted the words.

"I don't understand. Why'd he send those men after me at Last Chance?" Veronica asked. "If he was just biding his time…"

"Because he knew you weren't going to stop looking for your brother," Sydney said, her voice soft. "He wanted to move the game along. If you vanished, Wyatt must have thought that would sure grab Cale's attention."

"It would've grabbed it, all right," Cale muttered, eyes glinting.

Logan delivered the next bit of news, saying, "Then when Wyatt found out that federal agents were in town, he started to cover his tracks."

But she'd already figured that part out. The explosion at the sheriff's station…the men who'd been killed. Wyatt had done it all. He hadn't gone into the back in order to rescue Jimmy. He'd been getting an extra weapon, planning his kills, triggering the explosion.

Veronica glanced to the right. Jimmy stood, with his shoulders hunched and his chin down. The star on his chest gleamed dully. Jimmy wasn't speaking. He looked so dazed that she wasn't even sure he was hearing much of the conversation.

Jimmy's best friend had tried to kill him, had set him up for murder. The guy just didn't seem to have anyone he could rely on.

Veronica edged closer to Jimmy. When her fingers brushed against his arm, he flinched. His head snapped up, and he stared straight at her. "I didn't run you off the road, Ms. Veronica. That wasn't me!"

She nodded. "I know, Jimmy."

"I realized it was Wyatt. He brought my car in… had his gun… I asked him…asked if he'd hurt anyone…"

All eyes were on her and Jimmy.

"He said…he said he'd try again for you. That I could…could help him…" Jimmy shook his head. "That's not what I do. I don't hurt people, especially not good folks like you…."

She blinked away the tears that wanted to fill her eyes. Jimmy had always been so good, to everyone. "I know you don't do that, Jimmy."

His lips trembled. "You…you shouldn't have run to the car and tried to get me out. You should have left me."

Now Veronica was the one to shake her head. "That's not what I do," she said, giving him the same words back. "Especially not to good folks like you."

Some of the darkness seemed to leave Jimmy's eyes. He offered her a faint smile.

*We're going to be okay, Jimmy.* They'd both made it through the nightmare. They'd survived.

She felt a light touch on her shoulder. She turned and found Jasper staring at her with his stark gaze.

"You knew that Wyatt was going to take a shot at either me or Cale, didn't you?"

A frown pulled down her brows. "I knew he was going to shoot you both. First you, then Cale."

Jasper searched her eyes. "How'd you know who he'd go for first? Did he tell—"

"He knew that Cale loved me, so he trusted that my brother would never shoot, not when he thought I might be hurt." She was her brother's weakness. One that Wyatt had used. "And as for you..."

"He thought I didn't love you?" Jasper's words were flat.

She wasn't sure what to make of that sudden lack of emotion. Clearing her throat, Veronica said, "He wasn't sure if you'd hesitate as long. I wasn't sure so—"

His hands tightened on her. "Let me make you sure. I would *never* do anything to hurt you. For the rest of my life, I swear, I'll always protect you."

"And I'll always protect you," she told him quietly. "Why do you think I ran toward you?" To cover him, while her brother took the shot.

"You ran to me." He exhaled slowly. "Because you love me."

"Hell," Cale muttered. "This is it...my sister's about to—"

"And you love me," Veronica told him, lifting her chin and staring at him with all of the certainty she felt. "I didn't doubt that. Wyatt did. *His* mistake." A mistake that had cost the man his life.

Jasper pulled her closer against him. He acted as if no one else were in the room with them. Maybe to him, there wasn't anyone. She'd never had a man focus so completely on her that way before.

As if she were every dream that he'd ever had.

"I love you more than life," Jasper told her. His voice wasn't so flat anymore. Emotion rumbled in his words. "Hell, you *are* my life, Veronica. I might have screwed things up at the beginning, but from here on out, I'll be the man you need me to be. A man you can want—"

She rose onto her toes and kissed him. The silence around them was thick enough to slice. "You are the man I want." She smiled at him.

"He's gonna be in the family," Cale growled, sounding lost. "The EOD agent who hunted me down is gonna be in *my* family."

"Yes," Jasper said, and he smiled, too, a big, bright, happy smile that took Veronica's breath away. "I sure will be, *brother*." But then Jasper glanced over at Cale. "Only I won't be an EOD agent for much longer."

*What?*

Jasper's warm gaze turned back to her. "Seems that Whiskey Ridge could use a sheriff, and I know someone who could pull enough strings to get me that job."

"I'm good with strings," Logan added, offering a shrug.

Veronica knew her eyes had widened in surprise. "Y-you're staying here?"

"Is this where you'll be?"

A nod.

"Then this is the only place I want to be. We'll build our home together. Live together. Be *happy* here."

She wrapped her arms around his neck. "I'm happy wherever you are."

"Ah, damn," from Cale. "Get a room before I poke my eyes out." But she'd heard the happiness in her brother's voice. Cale just wanted her safe. He wanted her to be loved.

And he knew that Jasper loved her.

The danger was over. Time for the living and loving to begin. She had everything that she wanted right there in front of her, and Veronica wasn't about to let him go.

They'd survived a killer's deadly game. Now it was time for the happy ending that they both deserved.

Time for love and a new life.

Jasper took her hand and led her outside, away from the others. The rain had finally stopped. The sun shone down on them, lighting the town.

Jasper turned toward her. "I'm sorry, Veronica."

She stared back at him, her body held carefully still. "Sorry?"

"I wish I'd never lied to you. I wish I could go back and start things over."

"I don't want to go back." She didn't want to hear apologies or regrets. She much preferred it when he just talked about loving her. She stepped toward him, put her hands on his chest. "I just want to go forward, with you."

"It's so fast. What if you change your mind?"

He was afraid. Her big, tough ranger. Afraid he wasn't worthy of love. "Do you trust me, Jasper?"

"With my life."

The words had her heart beating faster. "Then trust me when I say that my mind won't change. I love you. I'll love you today." She leaned up. Kissed his lips. "And I'll love you for every tomorrow that comes."

His hands locked around her, so tight and strong. "I want you so much that the need I feel scares me."

"I think that's how love is supposed to be." Not perfect. Not gentle. But wild and dark and consuming. "Because that's the way I feel for you."

Not safe.

Not easy.

So much...so much it scared her, too.

Then his lips were on hers. He kissed her with a savage need. A need she felt for him, too. Finally, *fi-*

*nally* they were safe. Cale was clear. It wasn't about a mission or evidence or the EOD. It was just about them.

About the new life that they were going to start, together.

Scary, consuming…not perfect, but just what they both craved.

# Epilogue

Cale watched the sun as it slowly dipped below the horizon. It was so red, like blood in the sky. Seemed as if he spent most of his days covered in blood.

Killing.

Fighting.

"Why'd you save all those people?" The quiet question came from behind him. He tensed because he hadn't heard any footsteps approaching.

Cale looked over his shoulder. Sydney Sloan stood just a few feet away. She'd come out of the temporary headquarters without making so much as a sound. She stood with her hands on her slender hips, surveying him with a hooded gaze.

He forced a shrug. "Someone needed to save 'em. Why not me?"

She gave a little laugh. He watched her with care. Sydney Sloan was a beautiful woman, no doubt, but as an EOD agent, he knew the woman was also deadly. A man needed to be extra cautious around a woman like her.

He looked over her shoulder, didn't see her usual big, fierce EOD shadow, so he had to ask, "Where's Gunner?" Because from what he'd observed, he always seemed to be just a few steps away from Sydney.

She frowned at his question. Then she shrugged, but he didn't find the move to be as careless as she'd probably planned. "It would seem that most of your psych report was bull."

He nodded. "Most." His "aggressive tendencies"—yeah, that part had been true. He could get more than a little aggressive when the right circumstances occurred.

Like when someone was targeting his sister for death.

"The work you were doing on your own…it's not so different from what we do," Sydney said as she edged closer to him. "Rescuing people is part of our job."

"And hunting killers?"

"We do the work that no one else can." A deliberate pause. "You can believe that when someone targets EOD agents, *all* of us fight back."

Yeah, well, that was the reason he'd become number one on their hit list.

"Since Jasper's leaving, we'll have an opening on our team," she murmured. Her head cocked to the right as she studied him with that too-knowing gaze of hers.

He lifted a brow. "You're seriously offering me a job?"

"No."

The abrupt denial startled him.

"Logan's the one doing the offering. I'm just the messenger." Her smile widened, flashing a dimple in her cheek. "I guess he thought I might come across as friendlier. Especially when you consider that the other option was Gunner."

Gunner…the guy who looked as if he ate nails. The guy who watched Sydney with a fierce, protective stare.

"You are the better option," Cale agreed.

"So, are you interested?"

His gaze drifted away from her. He'd bought the place in Whiskey Ridge to try to give Veronica the stability that he knew she wanted. But she didn't need him or the land any longer, not really.

Cale had known the first time he saw Jasper look at Veronica that things had changed. During the time that he had served with Jasper in the military, the guy had *never* gazed at a woman with such desperate intensity. As if his whole world were in her hands.

But that was exactly the way he looked at Veronica. No, actually, Jasper looked at Veronica as if she were his entire world.

Things were changing now, and maybe it was time he changed some, too.

Working on his own—well, that had gotten him a close call with death. But with a team to back him up, with people he could count on...

Cale nodded. "I think I might be interested."

Sydney offered him her small palm. His fingers closed around hers. He shook her hand once. "Welcome to the team," she said.

*"Sydney."*

And there was another teammate. Gunner had just stepped outside, and he sure was glaring at Cale. Or rather, glaring at Cale's hand. The hand that was still holding Sydney's.

"Great news, Gunner," Sydney said as she pulled her hand free and looked back over her shoulder at the other man. "Cale's joining the team."

"Great," Gunner agreed, but he sounded anything but pleased. Then Cale met the other man's stare. Saw the very clear *don't touch* glare and got the picture.

He could join the team, but he needed to stay away from Sydney Sloan.

Message received.

Then Logan was there, closing out the team. His gaze swept over them. "We haven't tracked down the man who put out the hits on the EOD agents yet."

With both Wyatt and Reed Montgomery dead, that tracking sure would be harder.

"But we'll find him. The EOD doesn't stop."

"And we don't give up," Sydney said.

Gunner's gaze was on her. "No," he agreed, "we don't."

Cale couldn't wait for their next mission. He was ready to get back in action. He glanced back up at the sky. The streaks of blood-red were all but gone.

Maybe...just maybe...he'd be able to wipe off the blood from his own hands. One day.

His sister had gotten her happy ending.

*One day*...perhaps he'd get what he wanted, too.

* * * * *

# LARGER-PRINT BOOKS!
## GET 2 FREE LARGER-PRINT NOVELS PLUS
## 2 FREE GIFTS!

HARLEQUIN

# INTRIGUE

## BREATHTAKING ROMANTIC SUSPENSE

**YES!** Please send me 2 FREE LARGER-PRINT Harlequin Intrigue® novels and my 2 FREE gifts (gifts are worth about $10). After receiving them, if I don't wish to receive any more books, I can return the shipping statement marked "cancel." If I don't cancel, I will receive 6 brand-new novels every month and be billed just $5.24 per book in the U.S. or $5.99 per book in Canada. That's a saving of at least 13% off the cover price! It's quite a bargain! Shipping and handling is just 50¢ per book in the U.S. and 75¢ per book in Canada.* I understand that accepting the 2 free books and gifts places me under no obligation to buy anything. I can always return a shipment and cancel at any time. Even if I never buy another book, the two free books and gifts are mine to keep forever.

199/399 HDN FVQ7

| | |
|---|---|
| Name | (PLEASE PRINT) |

| | |
|---|---|
| Address | Apt. # |

| | | |
|---|---|---|
| City | State/Prov. | Zip/Postal Code |

Signature (if under 18, a parent or guardian must sign)

Mail to the **Harlequin® Reader Service:**
**IN U.S.A.:** P.O. Box 1867, Buffalo, NY 14240-1867
**IN CANADA:** P.O. Box 609, Fort Erie, Ontario L2A 5X3

**Are you a subscriber to Harlequin Intrigue books**
**and want to receive the larger-print edition?**
**Call 1-800-873-8635 today or visit www.ReaderService.com.**

\* Terms and prices subject to change without notice. Prices do not include applicable taxes. Sales tax applicable in N.Y. Canadian residents will be charged applicable taxes. Offer not valid in Quebec. This offer is limited to one order per household. Not valid for current subscribers to Harlequin Intrigue Larger-Print books. All orders subject to credit approval. Credit or debit balances in a customer's account(s) may be offset by any other outstanding balance owed by or to the customer. Please allow 4 to 6 weeks for delivery. Offer available while quantities last.

**Your Privacy**—The Harlequin® Reader Service is committed to protecting your privacy. Our Privacy Policy is available online at www.ReaderService.com or upon request from the Harlequin Reader Service.

We make a portion of our mailing list available to reputable third parties that offer products we believe may interest you. If you prefer that we not exchange your name with third parties, or if you wish to clarify or modify your communication preferences, please visit us at www.ReaderService.com/consumerschoice or write to us at Harlequin Reader Service Preference Service, P.O. Box 9062, Buffalo, NY 14269. Include your complete name and address.

HILP13

The series you love are now available in

# LARGER PRINT!

The books are complete and unabridged—
printed in a larger type size to make it
easier on your eyes.

⬧ HARLEQUIN®
*Romance*

**From the Heart, For the Heart**

⬧ HARLEQUIN®
**MEDICAL**™
*Pulse-racing romance,*
*heart-racing medical drama*

⬧ HARLEQUIN®
## INTRIGUE®
**BREATHTAKING ROMANTIC SUSPENSE**

⬧ HARLEQUIN®
*Presents*®

***Seduction and Passion Guaranteed!***

⬧ HARLEQUIN®
*super romance*®

***Exciting, emotional, unexpected!***

Try **LARGER PRINT** today!

Visit: www.ReaderService.com
Call: 1-800-873-8635

⬧ **HARLEQUIN**®

A *Romance* FOR EVERY MOOD™

www.ReaderService.com

HLPDIR13

# REQUEST YOUR FREE BOOKS!

## 2 FREE NOVELS
## PLUS 2 FREE GIFTS!

### WORLDWIDE LIBRARY®
#### Your Partner in Crime